REA

ALL...

P9-EEN-386

3 1...0 ...59 2459

Fiction
Ireland, Liz
Mom for a week

Ze...

that was about all Linda could muster at the moment. "Thank you, anyway, for trying to help."

In a second he was standing nose-to-nose with her. "You always could make up your mind fast. I've missed that about you, Lindy."

"That's not my name," she said, unable to tear her eyes away from his intense gaze.

"I'll always think of you as Lindy. Wild and Crazy Lindy, just like everybody called you." His voice dropped into a sexy whisper. "But only I knew exactly how wild you were, right, sweetheart?"

Linda's skin flamed. "I think you'd better go," she mumbled, turning away.

He kissed her briefly but fully. Stunned, Linda tripped forward. A crooked smile worked across his mouth. "Suit yourself," he said abruptly.

And then he was gone.

ROMAN...

Dear Reader,

Silhouette Romance rings in the New Year with a great new FABULOUS FATHER from bestselling author Elizabeth August! Murdock Parnell may be the *Ideal Dad* for eight-year-old Jeremy Galvin, but will he convince Jeremy's pretty mom, Irene, that he's her ideal husband?

In Kristin Morgan's latest book, Brianna Stansbury is *A Bride To Be*. Problem is, her groom-to-be is up to no good. It's up to Drew Naquin to rescue Brianna—even if that means marrying her himself!

Expectant Bachelor concludes Sandra Steffen's heartwarming WEDDING WAGER series about three brothers who vow they'll never say "I do." This time, Taylor Harris must battle the forces of love. And once he discovers the woman in his arms plans to be the mother of his child, it's not easy.

Rounding out the month, Carol Grace brings us a *Lonely Millionaire* who's looking for a mail-order bride. Liz Ireland turns up the laughter when a young woman finds herself playing *Mom for a Week*—with only her long-ago love to rescue her. And look for *The Man Who Changed Everything* from debut author Elizabeth Sites.

Until next month,

Happy reading!

Anne Canadeo
Senior Editor

Please address questions and book requests to:
Silhouette Reader Service
U.S.: 3010 Walden Ave., P.O. Box 1325, Buffalo, NY 14269
Canadian: P.O. Box 609, Fort Erie, Ont. L2A 5X3

MOM FOR
A WEEK

Liz Ireland

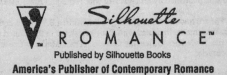

Silhouette
ROMANCE™
Published by Silhouette Books
America's Publisher of Contemporary Romance

If you purchased this book without a cover you should be aware that this book is stolen property. It was reported as "unsold and destroyed" to the publisher, and neither the author nor the publisher has received any payment for this "stripped book."

For Shatzie and Julia, my very own captive audience and critique duo. Thanks for listening to me whine, but most of all, thanks for never telling me to go home. Y'all are the best

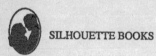 SILHOUETTE BOOKS

ISBN 0-373-19058-1

MOM FOR A WEEK

Copyright © 1995 by Elizabeth Bass

All rights reserved. Except for use in any review, the reproduction or utilization of this work in whole or in part in any form by any electronic, mechanical or other means, now known or hereafter invented, including xerography, photocopying and recording, or in any information storage or retrieval system, is forbidden without the written permission of the editorial office, Silhouette Books, 300 East 42nd Street, New York, NY 10017 U.S.A.

All characters in this book have no existence outside the imagination of the author and have no relation whatsoever to anyone bearing the same name or names. They are not even distantly inspired by any individual known or unknown to the author, and all incidents are pure invention.

This edition published by arrangement with Harlequin Enterprises B.V.

® and TM are trademarks of Harlequin Enterprises B.V., used under license. Trademarks indicated with ® are registered in the United States Patent and Trademark Office, the Canadian Trade Marks Office and in other countries.

Printed in U.S.A.

Books by Liz Ireland

Silhouette Romance

Man Trap #963
The Birds and the Bees #988
Mom for a Week #1058

LIZ IRELAND

lives in her native state of Texas, a place she feels provides a never ending supply of colorful characters. Aside from writing romance novels and tending to two very demanding cats and a guard dachshund, she enjoys spending time reading history or cozying up with an old movie.

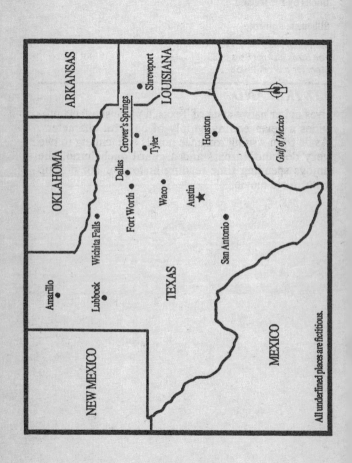

Chapter One

The blue eyes of two identical redheaded little boys squinted in June's bright morning sunlight, following Linda Potter as she nervously paced in front of her sister's wood-frame house. One of her nephews was sniffling, the other was just glaring. Clearly, they resented being left alone with their aunt for a whole week.

Last year, during her short visit home, one of them had bitten her on the leg. Unfortunately, she'd forgotten which one—she had never been around them long enough to tell them apart, a fact that made her very nervous now.

Every once in a while she could glimpse the one on the left taking a lick of his ice-cream cone when he thought she wasn't looking. She'd scooped up the cones as a sort of peace offering, but the boys seemed determined not to acknowledge her effort. The other one's cone hadn't even been touched—he was too busy crying to be hungry—and now the concoction was tilting dangerously, like a vanilla-chocolate-chunk Leaning Tower of Pisa.

Linda sighed and looked over the hedge bordering the property. What on earth was she going to do with herself in her old hometown for a week, with three children, no less!

Probably half of Grover's Springs already knew she was back in town, thanks to the supersensory capacities of her neighbors and an elaborate gossip network that reached from Mrs. Huckabee's house next door clear over to the Sit-n-Chat Beauty Parlor by the interstate. Growing up, Linda had never been able to fudge a curfew, sneak out on a school night, or throw a healthy, all-American, Dad's-out-of-town blowout party without getting caught.

Maybe because her father had been a minister, people had been a little more vigilant watching over her, she conceded. But even so, more than ten years later, the fact that she still had a preference for garish colors probably had been reported from house to house, along with the fact that she owned a flashy sports coupe and that she'd cut her hair in a short bob that entailed a close cropping of the hair on the back of her neck. She could imagine Mrs. Huckabee reporting to everyone that "Crazy Lindy" Potter had gone and gotten herself a burr.

Watch out, Linda could almost hear them say, *she's back.*

And probably most had heard by now that her sister, Naomi Ward, had been foolhardy enough to leave her baby and two boys in Linda's care. But no one could have been more shocked than Linda had been when she'd pulled into her sister's driveway for a short visit and had been greeted with the news that Naomi's father-in-law had died and that she and William needed to leave immediately—and that Linda was desperately needed to look after Saul and Seth, the almost-five-year-old twins, and little Emily, who had just turned six months. Cute children, but...

"But I don't know anything about kids!" she'd blurted out.

"No problem." Naomi, a natural mom, had waved off her sister's protest. "They practically run themselves."

"But—" A grim-faced William had moved past Linda with two suitcases. Weren't those bags rather large for a short trip? "It's just for a few days, right?" she'd asked. "I don't think the office can get along without me for too much longer—"

"Don't worry. We have to be back for the twins' birthday party on Saturday."

"Right," Linda had said, trying to glean hope from her sister's logical assertion. "I'm sure I'll do fine."

She'd been lying. She wasn't sure of anything, except that she owed it to Naomi to keep her upper lip stiff. Her practical, loyal, older sister had picked her up and dusted her off more times than she could count. Naomi had been Linda's biggest cheerleader when she'd decided to open her own travel agency two years before. In fact, it was no accident that Linda had chosen to visit Grover's Springs after an especially hectic week at the office.

June was always On the Wing's busiest month. In addition to managing their normally heavy business clientele, they had to deal with seemingly every family in the Dallas-Ft. Worth metroplex intent on descending upon Orlando, Florida. Lately she'd been considering opening a new branch office in Houston, but considering how long it took to get her first office off and running, she'd felt a migraine coming on just thinking about that!

So she'd left her "baby" in the competent hands of her trusted friend and assistant, Jane Cutler, and come to her old hometown, hoping to get some TLC from big sister. Instead, she was apparently about to get a crash course in Mothering 101. But she knew Naomi would never miss Saul and Seth's fifth birthday party on Saturday. Class would be over in a week.

Naomi and William hadn't gotten halfway down the block, when their old beat-up station wagon's brake lights had blinked on, and then the monster had begun backing up Sycamore Street.

"I forgot to tell you," Naomi had said through the open window, raising her voice above the engine's noise and the abandoned-child cries of one of the twins. "George Warren found somebody to send over to look at the washing machine. He'll be here within an hour."

Linda had recognized the name of the owner of the local hardware store and had nodded dumbly. Was Naomi trying to convey some hidden message to her? She'd felt almost as abandoned and desperate as the poor little boy who'd flung himself bodily at the car door.

"You'll need that washing machine," Naomi had said, patting the hysterical child's head and giving him a quick kiss. When Linda had looked at her questioningly, she'd explained, "Kids get dirty. Especially babies." After that alarming tidbit, the station wagon had roared off again, belching an ominous cloud of black smoke in parting.

That had been almost an hour ago. Linda was now a nervous wreck, but other than that, things were going smoothly, she thought as she did her five-minute inventory of the kids. Emily was parked in her perambulator on the porch, and the twins...well, at least they were all in one piece. So far, so good.

3 1833 02559 2459

After reaching the hedge, she pivoted toward the porch steps just in time to see a fat glob of chocolate ice cream blob down the front of one of the twins' shirts. With his free hand the boy in question wiped the chocolate down the front of his yellow T-shirt. His other hand still held fast to the gigantic cone. Which one was it, Saul or Seth? Linda vowed that she would be able to tell them apart by day's end.

The other twin scowled at her. His chocolate-coated brother looked from one to the other, then burst into tears.

"What happened?" Linda asked, running over.

"He thinks you're mad," the scowling boy said, crossing his arms as if to ask, *Are you?*

"But I didn't say a thing!"

Her rising voice only frightened the wailing child more, but when she reached toward him with a comforting hand, the boy howled as if he'd been stung by a malicious bee.

"He doesn't like for you to touch him." The other twin looked at her smugly. "Only Mommy."

Then what in tarnation was she supposed to do, Linda wondered, just stare helplessly while the kid cried?

She swore she caught a glimpse of Mrs. Huckabee peeking out her window next door. The woman, who hadn't spoken to Linda in a coon's age, was probably aghast that Naomi had left her with the children. But old Vera Huckabee probably still thought of her as the girl who ran through her prized pansy beds on Zeke Howell's motorcycle...and of course no one in town was ever likely to forget the night she and Zeke ran away to Mexico.

As always, the very thought of Zeke made Linda pause.

Although she and Zeke never actually made it past Waco, much less to the border, their wreck on the interstate had changed her life unalterably. She'd returned to Grover's Springs with her heart broken and her reputation in shreds. But, in a way, the incident had made her all the more determined to escape, and to make something of herself. By herself.

Linda always wondered where Zeke had escaped to. She hated to think that he still blamed her for their accident, the way everyone in Grover's Springs did. Linda had heard plenty of people whisper that she'd chased that young whippersnapper clear away. As in most small towns, people in Grover's Springs didn't forget.

Maybe that's why the place still brought out that reckless streak in her. Just being here made her want to do silly, childish things—the only speeding tickets she'd gotten in thirteen years had been in Grover's Springs.

But not this time, she vowed. Looking after these kids was the first favor Naomi had asked of her in years, and she was going to act like the thirty-year-old grown-up she was, even if it killed her. Only, what if something went wrong? Her knowledge of children was limited to what she had seen on TV commercials.

"Aunt Linda, Saul needs a tissue."

She looked down and tried to memorize the little faces. The red, puffy one on the left was Saul, then. She committed the information to memory. But what would happen when the face wasn't red and puffy anymore?

"Okay," she said, sure she had a goofy, obliging smile on her face. "I'll be right back."

Linda walked into the house, but no sooner had the squeaky screen door slammed shut behind her than she panicked. Was it okay to leave them alone on the porch for a few minutes? Ironically, it made her even more nervous to have them out of her sight than right in front of her, glaring.

She hurried through the house in search of a tissue, until the sudden sound of a long piercing whistle stopped her in her tracks. A shudder moved down her spine. Though she hadn't heard it in thirteen years, she knew that whistle all too well. It could mean only one thing.

Heart racing, Linda scanned the nearest bathroom for a tissue box, then quickly decided to take the obvious shortcut. She raced out of the house with a roll of toilet paper unraveling in her hand.

What she saw caused her to stop in mid-step. The screen door banged against her arm, but still she didn't move. A man knelt in front of the twins, talking to them in a low voice and mussing their red heads in a genial manner.

At the same moment that the man's dark blond hair came into focus, he seemed to notice that someone was on the porch, watching him. First, his gaze took in her feet—how could he miss them, encased as they were in hot-pink leather sandals? Then his gaze traveled slowly up her legs, pausing on her jet-black shorts, up the bright pink tank top that covered her torso and finally, with agonizing leisure, zeroed in on her neck, where her light pulse point beat wildly, both from the heat and from tension.

Slowly the man stood, and Linda's breath caught in a jolt of recognition.

He was taller than she remembered, perhaps six feet. And his build, once so wiry, had solidified into an impressive set of muscles—not stocky, but definitely the arms and chest of a man who worked at physical labor. His jaw was strong; it always had been, only now there was a harder cast to his mouth. But there was a relentless amused glint in his green eyes when Linda looked into them.

"Well," he said in that unforgettable low drawl, "if it isn't Crazy Lindy."

Nobody called her Lindy anymore—and especially not Crazy—or at least not to her face. It didn't suit the person she had become at all, and yet she couldn't imagine this man calling her anything but Lindy. Linda had to remind herself that she was a successful business-woman, just turned thirty, not a reckless teenager.

Because that's how she felt, just hearing Zeke Howell call her by name. Reckless.

"Zeke," she said, her voice barely audible even to her own ears. "What are you doing here?"

Zeke had known it was bound to happen sooner or later. Even though he'd heard Lindy Potter had moved to Dallas ages ago, it was natural that she would visit her sister. Hadn't he known that all along?

A little voice in the back of his mind countered, *Isn't that what you'd counted on all along?*

No, damn it! He'd gotten Lindy Potter out of his system years ago... round about the time she'd jilted him, he thought wryly. Besides, the chances that she'd be visiting on the only time he'd been called out to this house were almost nil.

It looked like his luck wasn't holding up too well.

But Lindy was. Through the years, Zeke realized, in the back of his mind he'd tried to imagine Lindy Potter growing old—flabby, wrinkly old, even if she was only thirty. Or maybe he'd hoped she would become a deter-mined old spinster, playing down her assets. When all else had failed, he'd tried to envision her as simply a crazy woman who wore army boots and kept cats.

One look dashed those hopes once and for all.

To say Lindy Potter hadn't changed at all would have been a lie—she'd changed, all right. She was more beautiful than ever. Not just in the way her body had matured into the ripe, luscious curves of a woman, either. She seemed taller than her old five foot five, but maybe that was simply because she held her narrow shoulders more proudly than he remembered. And the spark in her gray eyes held more challenge than defiance now.

He'd heard she'd become pretty successful, and a quick once-over verified that fact. Clothes that at first looked simply like her old flashy style, he realized upon second glance, had definitely not come off some department-store sale rack. And while she had shorn her once-luxuriously long hair, the jaunty haircut she now sported, with its soft angles accentuating her beautiful bone structure and long neck, was like something out of a magazine. In fact, every inch of Linda Potter bespoke a woman who was not to be tangled with.

Every inch, that is, except for the perfectly manicured hand that was nervously unwinding a roll of toilet tissue....

Zeke felt the corners of his mouth pulling into a comfortable old smile. He'd missed tangling with Lindy.

"What am *I* doing here?" he asked. "I live here. What's your excuse?"

Her chin jutted out defensively. "No one told me you moved back, Zeke."

His eyes widened in mock surprise. "You mean they took down the billboard on the interstate that said Welcome to Grover's Springs, Current Residence of Zeke Howell?"

Linda smirked. "I must have missed it. And I just got in today. Did you know I was here?" News did travel fast in this town.

"Actually, no."

Linda stared at him in confusion. "But you whistled." That was the old whistle he'd used to let her know he was waiting for her...usually when she was planning to sneak out after curfew.

"I was demonstrating for your nephews. You think I haven't whistled in all these years, Lindy?" Zeke asked, a touch of bitterness in his smile. "Although it was gratifying to see that you still come running so quickly."

Linda frowned. "Then what—"

"George told me you had a problem with your plumbing," Zeke answered for her.

Linda stared at him blankly for a split second before understanding dawned. She could feel a deep red flush crawling up her neck. "You mean—" She swallowed. "You're who George Warren was sending over?"

He graced her with a sarcastic little bow.

She'd just assumed he'd run over when he'd heard she was in town. Now she could kick herself. How stupid could she be? Given his choice, Zeke Howell would probably have avoided her like the plague.

Zeke nodded toward the toilet paper in her hands. "Any special reason you're dragging that around?"

Linda looked quickly down. "Oh! This was for Seth—I mean Saul. He was a little...uh, upset."

"Misses his mommy?"

His question elicited a fresh howl from the boy on the step in front of him. Linda threw up her hands in consternation. "I don't understand it. She's just been gone for a little over an hour."

"Hey, slugger," Zeke murmured soothingly, bending down on one knee and putting a firm hand on the boy's shoulder.

The twin's brother crossed his arms and turned a sour expression on Zeke. "His name's Saul, not slugger."

Zeke smiled and turned to Seth, never missing a beat. "Then you must be the slugger I've heard so much about."

The boy looked at him suspiciously. "Where'd you hear that?"

Zeke glanced up at Linda and winked. "This is a small town, you know," he said conspiratorially to the little boys. "People talk. Now what's the problem here?"

Linda could discern now that Saul was slightly smaller than his brother. Or maybe it just appeared that way when his tiny shoulders began to convulse.

"Mommy and Daddy left us," he blurted out miserably, "with—with mean Aunt Linda!"

Linda's jaw fell slack. *Mean? Her?* How could that be? She caught Zeke's gaze and pleaded innocently, "I just got here."

"She made a face when Saul spilled ice cream," Seth piped up. He shot her a defiant little glare that almost made Zeke laugh. It was a Linda Potter glare, nascent but unmistakable.

"Are you sure about that?" Zeke asked.

Linda couldn't believe she was letting a man she hadn't seen for thirteen years step into a sticky domestic situation. Since when had Zeke Howell, man on a bike, become a child-care expert?

Sensing he was about to be told where to get off, Zeke sent Linda a look that said "Trust me." She might have gained experience in all sorts of things over the years, but apparently none of it had to do with kids.

"First of all," he said, looping an arm around Seth's shoulder, "I bet your mom wouldn't want you to be sad the whole time she's gone, now would she?"

Burying his fists in his cheeks, the boy stubbed his tiny sneaker against the porch step and slowly, grudgingly, shook his head. "I guess not," he admitted.

"Uh-uh," his twin agreed.

"I didn't think so," Zeke said. "And as for being dumped with your aunt here—" he raised an eyebrow toward Linda "—you fellas don't know how good you've got it."

Linda watched as the back of both small heads slowly lifted, then turned toward her in unison. The expressions on the identical faces were skeptical.

"Why, your aunt's practically a celebrity in this town."

"Zeke!" So that was his game! Seeking long-denied revenge, he was going to use the twins to get her riled up.

He ignored her. "I bet you kids didn't know that mean old Aunt Lindy here is probably the best dancer this town's ever seen."

"Aunt Linda?" Seth asked, disbelieving.

"Zeke Howell, I'm warning you—"

"Absolutely," Zeke said. His eyes gleamed with mischief, and Linda knew why. The last time he'd seen her dancing was in the middle of the night in the Cornelius Grover fountain in Grover's Springs municipal park! She'd been doing a spirited rendition of "Girls Just Wanna Have Fun," when someone—Vera Huckabee, she more than suspected—had called the police. Linda had been dragged away, sopping wet, for creating a public nuisance.

"Your aunt has all sorts of hidden talents," Zeke concluded with a wink for Linda alone.

Seth and Saul looked up at her, and although their expressions didn't relay anything like admiration or complete trust, they at least weren't hostile. It was a beginning.

Linda crossed her arms. That she owed this small victory to Zeke Howell seemed the height of irony. For years she'd kept her visits to Grover's Springs to a minimum, in part to avoid hearing about Zeke—or even speculation about him. Now, here he was, bailing her out of her first crisis after only one hour in town on her own.

"Thanks, I guess," she said, squaring her shoulders.

He stood in that leisurely way Linda remembered so well. She found it hard to keep her eyes from exploring his chest, his arms. Instead, she forced herself to focus on his green eyes, but to her dismay she discovered that they held her transfixed, half in memory and half in the awkward present.

What was she supposed to say? "Now that you've fixed it with my nephews, can you try the washing machine?" This was Zeke, not a stranger, not some impersonal Mr. Fixit sent over by old George Warren. And yet, he *was* a stranger. Thirteen years could change a person, as it had her. She couldn't speak to him as if nothing had happened.

Suddenly the memory of their last meeting flashed through her mind. Zeke, in a hospital room, his leg in a cast. His eyes looking up at her, taking in the measly little sling supporting her left arm. A sprain, the doctor had said. It seemed so minor in comparison to Zeke's injury. His femur had been crushed by the motorcycle during the accident.

His bike, needless to say, had been totaled. Perhaps that was why he had looked at her with such accusation.

"Go home, Lindy," he'd said finally.

"But how? Zeke, I—"

He interrupted her. "Easy. Call Daddy."

"But my father will ki—"

"No he won't," Zeke bit out. "He'd probably rather kill me."

"Oh, Zeke, I'm not going to leave—"

"Call him, Lindy."

His tone had been so adamant, so embittered, that she'd left the room. Her last impression of Zeke had been of his face, his mouth set in a determined line, staring out the window at the bleak hospital parking lot. Of course, being seventeen and seeing no alternative, Linda had headed straight for a telephone.

In the days that had followed, stifled by the stern disapproving eye of her father, she'd wanted to call Zeke, to visit. But he'd made it clear that he didn't want to have anything to do with her. Then, when her father had had a heart attack only a week later, Zeke's rebuff had stung all the more. Had she caused her father so much stress over a man who hadn't even cared for her?

As she explored the planes of his face in the hot June sunshine, she took in a few weathered lines around the eyes and the deep laugh lines around his mouth. His was a face that had seen things, just as he'd always said he would. That she hadn't been with him struck her suddenly with sadness.

He took a deep breath. "Have I checked out to your satisfaction?"

Linda felt a blush creep up her neck. "I'm sorry," she apologized. "It's been so long. I guess I was staring."

Zeke let out a heavy sigh, suddenly feeling self-conscious and, by comparison to the woman next to him, maybe a little shabby. He'd always thought Lindy had it all. A good family name, beauty, money. Those things were a triple threat to a guy like him, and now she had them in spades. No wonder she was giving him the once-over with that imperious gaze of hers. She probably hadn't spoken to someone of his ilk in years.

Probably not since she'd said good riddance at that hospital in Waco, he thought bitterly. That was still the low point of his life—lying flat in a hospital bed, already worried about paying the damned hospital bill and then realizing that he had absolutely nothing to offer Linda Potter.

Just an adventurous spirit—but she'd fled from that quickly enough, hadn't she?

"If you've finished your examination, you might as well show me whatever needs fixing."

"It's the washing machine." Linda swallowed. Why was he being so curt? "Zeke, when did you start working for George Warren?"

He raised an eyebrow. "Isn't that a kind of personal question?"

He was kidding her, she knew, but there was grit in his tone. "When did you come back to Grover's Springs?" she asked.

He squinted against the sun. "I didn't mean to move in on your territory. In fact, they told me you never come back to town. Sorry, sweetheart, if it makes you uncomfortable."

His words, especially the sarcastic *sweetheart,* stung. She didn't know what she'd done to deserve this rancor, but Zeke Howell wasn't the only one with pride. "I'm sure you can move wherever you want."

"Thanks. I do remember growing up here, if that gives me a right to call the old place home. Of course my father was just the town drunk, not a minister or anything like that."

He shifted sullenly to his other foot and regarded her with a fathomless gaze. Years ago they'd argued down this winding path. He'd baited her for being a minister's daughter, never letting his own dad off the hook, either. But now there was scant humor in his tone.

"Our fathers are gone, Zeke. Anyway, we don't want to start this up," Linda said.

"No, we don't," he replied. "Or were you using the 'royal' we?"

Linda lifted her chin and regarded him through narrowed eyes. Apparently he was carrying around some residual bitterness. But what about her? Hadn't he ever wondered about her side of the story—about having to hold her head up in town for a year, until she escaped to college? Did he even know that her father had suffered a heart attack only a week after he'd picked her up from that hospital? Probably not. Anyway, no man would understand the guilt she felt for causing her father that much stress.

Suddenly she was seized with indignation. She was in town now for only a week. She and Zeke didn't need to see each other at all. It would be easy enough to find someone else to fix the washing machine, and they could both let the past bury itself.

"Actually, Zeke, Naomi called George before I got here. I haven't even had time to look at the machine myself. Maybe she was being hasty."

"Hasty." Zeke rubbed his chin thoughtfully before looking back at her. "Meaning, you want me to get lost."

"I'd like the chance to look it over," Linda said, feeling as if a partially healed crack were reopening in her heart. Zeke deserved better than a curt dismissal, but that was about all she could muster at the moment. "Thank you, anyway."

In a second he had climbed the few steps to stand nose-to-nose with her. "You always could make up your mind fast. I've missed that about you, Lindy."

"That's not my name," she said, unable to tear her eyes away from his intense gaze. A knot formed deep in her belly.

He hooked a hand around the porch support next to her. "I'll always think of you as Lindy. Lucky Lindy. Wild and Crazy Lindy, just like everybody called you." His voice dropped into a sexy whisper. "But only I knew exactly how wild you were, right, sweetheart?"

Linda's skin flamed. "I think you'd better go," she mumbled, turning away.

His strong fingers cupped her chin and swiveled her face back around. His green eyes mesmerized her; she couldn't look away again.

"I traveled," he said. "I went all over this damn continent, just like we said we would do together. But I never found anyone like you, Lindy. Never." His head bent closer, until she could feel his breath on her lips as he spoke. "I never found anything half as sweet as this."

Their lips joined briefly but fully. Stunned, Linda tripped forward, and Zeke used her loss of equilibrium to pull her closer. There was no mistaking the taut edge of desire she felt rippling through his muscles or the excitement of her own quickening pulse.

They weren't teenagers anymore, that much was certain.

"Zeke," she said breathlessly, pulling away.

A crooked smile worked across his mouth. Even white teeth gleamed in the sultry shade of the porch. Behind them, baby Emily let out a worried coo. God only knew what the twins were doing, or what they were thinking. For all her bravado, Linda was too much of a coward to look.

"Suit yourself," Zeke said abruptly.

Linda stared at him, uncomprehending. "What?"

He shrugged. "About the washing machine. If you want to take a look at it first, suit yourself."

Linda stepped back, wiping her brow. How had he changed gears so quickly? Already he was stepping down from the porch, while she was still struggling to catch her breath. He turned to the twins once more.

"Be nice to your aunt, sluggers," he said. "She's more delicate than she looks."

With a wink he turned and moved toward the street with his signature ambling gate. It was uneven, Linda noted, favoring one leg. He turned back when he reached the hedge and yelled at her in a voice the whole neighborhood could hear.

"See you around, Crazy Lindy!"

Linda closed her eyes as he disappeared behind the foliage. She heard him slam the door, start the truck and roar off down the street.

Wild? Crazy? She felt wild, all right. Unfortunately she also felt like a class-A sap. He'd played her for a fool, making her practically swoon in his arms right there for all of Sycamore Street to see, teasing her with words he must have known would seduce her completely. Yet the kiss had meant nothing to him.

Through the corner of her eye, she could just make out the rustling of Mrs. Huckabee's kitchen curtain.

"C'mon guys, let's go in."

"Is Zeke coming back?" Seth asked. Saul looked up just as expectantly as his brother. "We like *him*."

Linda shepherded the boys through the screen door before wheeling Emily in after them. "I don't think so."

Not if she had any say in the matter. She would call a plumber in from Dallas, if she had to, rather than allow Zeke Howell to humiliate her. Again.

Chapter Two

Linda was still recovering from her encounter with
Zeke, when she realized, in one blinding moment, the
depth of the crisis she had on her hands.

As she flipped through the phone book looking for
plumbers, she heard Emily crying. Maybe it was catch-
ing. She could still hear Saul sniveling in the next room.

Gingerly Linda peeked over the baby carriage where
her niece had been sleeping soundly only moments before. Nothing looked wrong—at first. Going down her
mental checklist of possible baby woes, Linda did the
obvious and pulled back Emily's blanket. What she discovered terrified her.

Cloth diapers!

Small wonder Naomi had sounded so emphatic about
fixing the washing machine. Linda envisioned a week's
worth of soiled diapers stacking up through the house.
What was she going to do? She had to get that washing
machine fixed! Soon!

Not only that, but she had to change her niece. That was a whole other problem in itself. Linda worried her lip as she carried Emily upstairs. Behind her she could hear curious whispers and the light footfalls of her nephews.

Linda could work out her company's taxes in no time and finagle a deal with the cagiest businessman in Texas. But faced with the pale colors of Emily's baby-powder-scented nursery, she felt as helpless as the child clinging so trustingly to her.

For a moment Linda closed her eyes and tried to reach deep inside to that place all women were supposed to have inside them—that magical font of maternal knowledge. Even though she'd never had to change a diaper or burp a squirming little bundle in her entire life, she'd always assumed the mothering instinct would kick in as needed. When she opened her eyes, however, she was as clueless as before. Maybe her maternal font had sprung a leak.

"Mommy keeps stuff in there," Seth offered after a long silent moment, pointing to a closet.

Linda nodded. "Thank you, Seth." At least, she assumed that one was Seth, since he wasn't crying. Spotting a table with a Formica top, she deposited the baby so she could inspect the closet.

Baby wipes. Pins. Soft, folded squares of cotton Linda assumed were the laundered diapers. She grabbed an armful of supplies and hurried back to the changing table. Seth had hauled over a chair and stepped up to inspect her technique.

Linda almost laughed. Technique was the least of her worries. If only Naomi used disposables, the box might have come with instructions! The stacks of thick cotton diapers Linda found in the baby's room were decadently soft, but frankly, they stumped her. She hadn't grappled with a problem like this since her baby doll clogged up back in the late sixties.

"She's stinky," Seth said. Saul, still hanging back in the doorway, nodded and wiped his nose with the back of his hand.

Trying to memorize the process in reverse, Linda slowly undid the diaper. *Now what?* She guessed she was supposed to start the cleaning procedure, but exactly what that should entail, she wasn't entirely certain.

She hazarded a glance at Seth. His pudgy elbows were propped on the tabletop and his nose was wrinkled dramatically. Suddenly an idea struck her. One of the most important things one learned in management seminars was to optimally utilize the knowledge of one's employees. These boys probably had a wealth of useful information inside those little red heads.

She recalled the firm but gentle tone Zeke had used with them. She didn't know where he'd learned it, or how, but she attempted to mimic it precisely. "I bet you and your brother would love to help," she said, frowning at the saccharine way the words came out of her mouth.

The child's eyes widened, and he appeared to think for a moment. "No, thanks," he said spiritedly. "I want my MTV!"

"Me, too!" Saul echoed enthusiastically, a hearty sniff the only sign of his earlier melancholy.

Rock videos? For four-year-olds? "Hey—"

Before Linda could protest, Saul and Seth abandoned her, their small feet tromping noisily down the steps. MTV?

Linda looked at Emily, naked and gently flailing on her back on the table. She couldn't run after the twins while their sister was just lying here, but what would Naomi say if she came back and her kids were running around singing heavy metal songs?

Relax, she suddenly thought. *You grew up listening to Donna Summer moaning "Love to Love You, Baby." You thought it was a lullaby.*

Only slightly reassured, she turned back to Emily. Now what?

As her waist brushed against the counter, she felt the comforting presence of her beeper. She looked up at the telephone. Jane, of course!

Linda rushed over to the phone on the stand next to the crib and dialed the numbers to the office. Jane Cutler was a wonder. On top of being her oldest employee, she was also a friend and the most knowledgeable person Linda knew. If Jane didn't know something, she always knew where to find out about it, which usually was from among her host of relatives.

Jane answered the phone with a crisp hello.

"Jane, this is Linda." She could envision her friend smiling and snapping to attention at the other end. It was a soothing image. There were actually some people in this world who took Linda seriously, even if she had to pay them to do so.

"Nothing's wrong, I hope," Jane said, concerned.

"Uh, maybe not. I've somehow wound up temporarily in charge of my sister's kids."

"No problem," Jane said. "I know all about kids. That happens when you have five little sisters."

At the sound of Jane's cool, competent voice, Linda felt herself smile. The woman was a wonder. "All I need to know right now is how to change a diaper."

"Are you kidding me? That's easy," Jane chirped, and began to rattle off instructions.

"Wait!" Linda pulled the phone back to the changing table. The cord just barely reached, so that her head had to jut at an awkward angle to talk and change at the same time. "This is hands-on training."

Twenty minutes later Linda had a finished product on her hands that both she and Emily could be satisfied with. "Anything to report on the office?" she asked, already feeling more relaxed.

"Just this," Jane said in the same self-assured tone she'd used while telling Linda exactly when to fold what where. "Someone from Advantage Microchips called in response to the letter we sent out. They said they're casting about for a new agency."

"We need to follow up. Put that down for me to do later in the week, and I'll mark it, too. Anything else that needs my attention?" Linda hated being away from the office for any length of time.

"Not really." Jane's reply was followed by silence.

"No messages?" Linda asked. Surely *something* required her attention.

"Not a thing," Jane assured her.

Linda's heart sank. Her agency, On the Wing, not need her? She'd spent two years with that company, two years without a vacation of any note that wasn't a business trip, and now it seemed that four salaried employees could run the place just fine.

"If you do need me, I can probably pack up the kids and be in Dallas in a heartbeat," Linda said anxiously. To be in Dallas, in her familiar apartment, miles and miles away from her lingering attraction to Zeke Howell....

"Kids do better in their own space," Jane countered. "Just relax, Linda. Enjoy the vacation—and your niece and nephews."

But Linda barely knew them—that was also what had come of devoting her life to her business. Not for the first time she wondered if she'd been a bit too focused on her career. But how could she be otherwise, when she had a business to run?

"Okay," Linda said, trying to keep the shakiness out of her voice.

"If you have any problems, give me a call." Jane laughed. "Just remember, be firm."

"Firm," Linda repeated. Firm wasn't her strong suit.

"But not too firm," Jane added hastily. "Indulge them. You're their aunt. Besides, kids like to think they have some power."

"Indulgent, but firm." The words came out in a fearful monotone. This was going to be a disaster.

Nevertheless she hung up feeling slightly more positive after making contact with the outside world. It was good that she didn't have to worry about the business, she reminded herself. Wasn't that what gave her the luxury of considering opening a new office in Houston?

However, she still had the washing machine dilemma to deal with. Without further ado, she picked up Emily and returned downstairs to call a plumber. The two boys joined her at the kitchen table as she walked her fingers through the phone listings.

"What are you doing, Aunt Crazy?"

Linda frowned. She'd heard that children were like little sponges, never missing a trick, and here was proof. She mentally lambasted Zeke for his insistence on using her hated nickname.

"Aunt *Linda*," she corrected. "And I'm looking for a plumber."

There were three plumbers in Grover's Springs. She started with Bernie Sharp, whom she remembered as being a genial older man. Bernie first registered surprise at hearing from Linda of all people, then listened sympathetically to her problem.

After hearing the saga of the washing machine, however, his first words were, "You mean Naomi left *you* in charge of those kids?"

So much for seeking out kind old men, Linda thought. "Do you think you can fix the washing machine, Mr. Sharp?"

"I'm sorry, Lindy," he said. "I've got to snake out the drains at the Palmer house today, and then we've got a big job at the Alton place that should take us till the end of the week."

"Oh." Linda tried to keep the despair out of her voice. "So you probably wouldn't be able to get to me until the weekend?"

"I'm sorry," Bernie repeated. "But I've got a hunch that the problem isn't too bad. For that kind of job, you'd do just as well to get George to send Zeke Howell over."

A tense silence followed as Bernie remembered who it was he was talking to. "Hmm. Or maybe you wouldn't want to do that."

And so it went with the other two people she called. It was as if the entire town had sprung a leak—or all the plumbers were conspiring against her. None could take the time to fix a piddling thing like a broken washing machine before the weekend, and everyone thought she should just get Zeke.

She'd sooner wash a million soiled diapers by hand than submit herself to more insults from him, though. Already the whole town probably knew that he'd kissed her right there in broad daylight on her sister's porch steps!

Instinctively she rubbed the back of her hand over her lips, remembering in minute detail every split second of their brief kiss. It wasn't only his sensuality that shocked her—it was her own response. How could a man have such an effect on her after all these years?

And how could she avoid being so exposed in future?

Obviously the only solution was to fix the machine herself. The idea seemed daunting at first, but less so the more Linda thought about it. After all, she had earned her MBA at night school. How hard could fixing a little machine be?

George Warren was agitated. Or as agitated as Zeke imagined the old fellow got these days.

"Still reroofing that house of yours?" George asked anxiously.

"No, the Bledsoes' roof needed patching up." His own was finished, thank goodness.

George hovered at the opening of the aisle Zeke was standing in, his ever-present pipe gently wafting blue smoke to mix with the homey smell of cut lumber. The old man usually kept to his perch in front of the old cash register, surveying his store through narrowed eyes as if he expected all the nails, ropes and tubes of rubber cement to up and march out the door someday.

Zeke was probably one of the few people in town who knew that nothing would have made George happier. Ever since Zeke had come back to town five months ago, George had constantly pestered him to come into the business with him so he could have more time for his one passion in life—fishing.

Zeke wasn't sure he was interested, though he would like to help George out. The old guy had given him his first job and had been like a father to him in the old days. He'd also been the first to welcome him back, even recommending him as a handyman to people who came into the store. He drummed up most of Zeke's business, and in return Zeke's repairs made for faithful customers. Not that George had much competition.

But Zeke was having a hard enough time dealing with his decision to settle in Grover's Springs; he couldn't decide just yet whether he wanted to be saddled with a store, too. Owning a business wouldn't leave him much time for his true passion, restoring old homes. But then, it would provide him with the money he needed for that work.

Usually George didn't press the issue. Today, though, he looked as if he were on pins and needles. Zeke picked up the box of nails he needed and walked to the front of the store.

George shuffled to his place behind the counter but waved Zeke away when he took out his wallet.

"I've got to pay you something, George," Zeke protested. "Your going out of business won't do me any good, you know."

George shook his head emphatically. "Call it repayment for sending you out to the Wards' place," he said. "I heard about the set-to you had with that Potter woman."

Zeke rolled his eyes. "It wasn't exactly a set-to."

The old man harrumphed. "Vera Huckabee said that woman practically threw herself at you."

"What?" Zeke couldn't believe news traveled so fast—and so inaccurately.

A gray, bushy eyebrow arched up eagerly. "Was she really wearing a hot-pink micromini?"

Just hearing those strange words coming out of George's mouth made Zeke laugh out loud. "They were shorts, George. Not even short shorts."

The older man's shoulders slumped a little in disappointment. "You just can't trust that Vera," he said, drawing on his pipe. "She's been wearing the same bifocals for twelve years."

Zeke shook his head. He should have known. Linda Potter's visit to town was big news. That she had actually spoken to him of all people probably warranted an emergency bulletin.

"She didn't want me to fix the machine, by the way."

"So you did talk to her." George leaned forward. "Are you sure that wasn't a miniskirt?"

"For God's sake, George!" Zeke exclaimed. "What's up with you and Vera, anyway? You two spend half your time gossiping together these days!"

"Mind your own business." George shuffled to his familiar place behind the counter, a worried expression on his face. "That Potter girl's a bad one to tangle with, in case you don't remember," he warned, hoisting himself onto a tall stool.

Zeke had to stifle a laugh. "She's not a girl anymore, George."

George slapped his hand on the counter. "Even worse!"

"And as far as that goes, I'm not exactly a kid, either." Zeke sent the older man a stern look.

George narrowed his eyes on Zeke, picked up a mangled yellow pencil and jabbed the air with it as he spoke. "You might not be a kid, but you ain't thinking like an adult, neither."

"I—"

"Nah, don't bother trying to make excuses. I haven't forgotten how that girl had you all tore up in knots way back when, even if you have. She encouraged you to run around thinkin' all kinds of foolish things, like running off to Mexico and seein' the world."

"Yeah, and that's what I did."

"Humph. Not with her, you didn't." A gray, bushy eyebrow shot up sagely. "And you landed yourself in a hospital first."

Zeke folded his arms across his chest. As if he needed to be reminded! The memory of how it felt to have Lindy reject him at the first sign of trouble was still as raw as if it had just happened yesterday. George was a fool if he thought he'd set himself up for that kind of torment again.

"That was an accident, George. Accidents happen. There is absolutely nothing newsworthy going on between Lindy and me. And there isn't going to be." He punctuated this declaration by slamming down two dollars on the counter.

George took the money and punched the keys to the old cash register. The drawer flew open with an alert ring. "So that kiss Vera was tellin' me about...that was just an accident, too."

"That's right," Zeke said emphatically, trying not to visualize the incident George had brought up. He'd spent hours already trying to avoid reliving the memory of that kiss and how soft Lindy had felt in his arms.

George chuckled. "I can just see it. You're standing there, she's standing there—maybe in a tiny little skirt—and boom! All of a sudden you accidentally start kissing."

Zeke felt his face heat up. "What's the matter, George? You worried Lindy Potter's going to ruin your plans to spend the rest of your life fishing?"

"Dad gum, Zeke!" George exclaimed, letting him know that he, too, had hit a nerve. "That Potter woman's no good for you."

But Zeke knew that it wasn't Lindy who was dangerous. It was his reaction to her. "I wouldn't worry, George," he said, reassuring the older man. "I came back here because Grover's Springs is the only place I knew of to call home. Lindy Potter doesn't even live here, so I don't see how she can chase me off."

His words did more than reassure—they absolutely got George's hopes up. "That offer of mine still stands, Zeke," he said excitedly, launching into his weekly pitch at last. "This old scrap heap might not look like much to you, but it's the only hardware store on this side of the county."

George had reminded him of that fact a thousand times already. "I'll keep it in mind," Zeke said.

The frown on George's face as he looked out the front window made Zeke nervous. "Humph. Speak of the devil," George said, just before the bell above the entrance jangled.

Zeke immediately followed George's gaze, which was focused on the woman coming through the door. Or attempting to. Lindy Potter was having a time of it, angling a baby stroller through the heavy glass door. Especially when the twins attempted to take a shortcut inside the store through her legs. The bell rang noisily every time Linda moved. The sound didn't impede her progress, exactly, but it was clearly getting on her nerves.

One of the boys, still trying to negotiate his way around his aunt, spotted Zeke and pointed with a stubby little finger.

"Look, Aunt Lindy, it's your boyfriend!"

Linda looked up just in time to see Zeke's expression change from one of bemusement to a mortification that she was sure matched her own.

"Zeke!"

"It's Sluggo!" the other brother chimed.

The two boys nearly knocked Linda clear off her feet in their zeal to maneuver around her and pounce on their new friend.

"Whoa, fellas," Zeke said, barely able to hold the twins at bay. "Didn't you know that gentlemen are supposed to hold the door open for a lady?"

The twins' heads turned in unison. "You mean Aunt Linda?"

"Prettiest lady in the entire hardware store," Zeke said with a smile, as he held the door and tried to tug the stroller through.

At the same time, annoyed by Zeke's sarcastic jibe—it was apparent from his tone that she was the *only* woman there—Linda gave the infernal buggy a final push and nearly fell across the threshold.

"And I've heard that ladies are supposed to say thank you," Zeke told the children, directing a laughing glance her way.

"Thanks," Linda snapped back crisply, careful not to let her gaze linger long on his deep green eyes. Even after thirteen years, the man affected her like a drug.

"Don't mention it," Zeke said. He couldn't help noticing that she'd changed into a pair of jeans that came to a tight peg at her calves, espadrilles and a crocheted shirt over a tank top. In spite of the stylishness of her little outfit, it was mussed enough to show that she'd been up to something.

As if in answer to his unspoken question, one of the twins piped up boastfully, "Aunt Lindy's gonna fix our washing machine all by herself."

"Oh, no."

Zeke hadn't meant to voice his reaction, and he could tell by the way Lindy's head snapped up and her gray eyes burned into his that she was mad as a hornet.

"Do you have a problem with that?" she asked.

Zeke took in her disparaging look and realized in a second what it was about the old Lindy that was missing—her sense of fun. Oh, he'd seen fleeting glimpses of it in her tart responses, but what had happened to the girl who'd danced with such abandon that night in the Cornelius Grover fountain? Had someone drained the spirit out of her on her way to becoming a woman and successful businesswoman?

"It's not my problem that's in question here," he said after a moment's thought.

"Well, I for one feel confident that I can fix that machine." It was just her luck that she would run into Zeke Howell twice in one day, Linda thought. Although of course he and George Warren had always been close. She should have seen this coming.

She turned to the shopkeeper, who looked exactly the same as she remembered. It was as if he hadn't moved from his same old perch in thirteen years. "I'm sure you don't mind if I look around for what I need, do you, Mr. Warren?"

The old man's eyes widened innocently as he sucked on his pipe. "No, no," he said. Then, mumbling, he added, "Just hope there aren't any accidents."

Linda hesitated, then shrugged off that ominous-sounding comment. People in this town always kept her off balance somehow. "C'mon, kids," she said to the twins, who were beginning to uncoil a length of rope, "we need to look for our stuff."

Zeke watched them obediently follow, then fell into line himself. It was as if Linda had him by a lead, he thought, frowning to himself in silent warning. But he couldn't help himself. He had to know.

"What's wrong with it?" he asked.

Linda turned. For a moment he caught a doubtful look in her eye, then she smiled self-assuredly. "It's the pipes," she declared.

"Uh-oh," George muttered.

Pipes? The woman was headed for certain disaster.

"Anything I can help you with, Ms. Potter?" George Warren asked, throwing Zeke a dubious look.

She unfolded a piece of paper and leaned against the stroller. "Uh, I have a list, with measurements. I believe I can find everything," she said with just a hint of a waver in her voice.

This was just too much, Zeke thought as he watched Linda going over her list. Why should they go on with this impersonal charade? She needed his help, and he was more than willing to lend a hand. What was so difficult about that?

His mind flashed back to that morning. Her gray eyes had darkened in that split second before he took her in his arms. He could remember the exact feel of her, the scent of her hair, the way her lips opened in surprise.

There might be a few difficulties, after all, he thought. Like how to keep his hands off her.

When Zeke looked back at Linda, her brows were knit together worriedly as she perused the shelf in front of her—it was obvious she didn't know what she was doing. He dug his hands into his pockets and pushed past the mops and brooms on her aisle.

"Tell you what," he offered. "Why don't I buzz by your house this evening and take a look?"

Linda nibbled her lip and thought over his tempting offer. She had been so certain, when she left the house, that the problem was the pipes; now she wasn't so sure. She couldn't let Zeke Howell know that, however.

"No, I think I've pinpointed the problem," she said, shaking her head. "It's the pipes. And those little hose things."

"Which one?" Zeke asked, unable to resist challenging her.

"All of them."

"Lord 'a mercy!" cried George from somewhere behind them.

Zeke shifted his weight and tried very hard to keep his face a mask of calm. Damn, she was stubborn. Clearing his throat again, he said quietly, "I don't know if you're aware of this, but it's pretty rare for everything to give out all at once."

"No, I didn't know that." She thumbed through different packages of sandpaper as though she had never seen such fascinating objects before.

Zeke shifted again and asked, "Are they leaking?"

"The pipes?" Linda asked innocently. "I think so."

"You *think* so? You're not sure they're leaking and you're going to replace them?"

Linda turned on him with barely leashed fury. Surely Zeke knew how much her coming into George Warren's hardware store had cost her. The man had never liked her, and now Zeke was making her look like a complete fool—again—when she was only doing this to avoid him to begin with.

"I'm doing this as a preventative measure," she said. "If you'd just let me—"

She held up a hand to silence him. "I've got this under control, Zeke. Thanks."

Even as she said the words, a nagging worry was beginning to eat at her. Maybe Zeke was right. But no. She remembered how bitter he'd been that morning. Zeke was probably just trying to scare her half to death, perhaps in retaliation for what had happened all those years ago. Wasn't that the way of the world? Through the ages, men had gotten even with the opposite sex by inventing things women didn't know how to fix.

Zeke frowned. It was obvious the woman had made up her mind that she wanted nothing more to do with him. Fine. But he couldn't resist saying, "Shouldn't you be a little worried about learning how to be a Ms. Fixit on your sister's major home appliances?"

Linda squared her shoulders. "Why should I be, since I'm confident I can fix it?" she asked with an imperious smile.

George cleared his throat. "Should I show you what you need, Lindy?"

"Thank you, Mr. Warren," she said, following the older man. In the corner of her eye, she saw Zeke watch her, then turn to leave. The jangle of the door made her sigh with relief that she'd survived another encounter with him.

But it also made her feel sad. And a little mystified. Why hadn't she simply accepted his help? He was right in that sense. She shouldn't let her pride wreck her sister's machine.

On the other hand, she knew it wasn't just her pride at stake. Seeing Zeke was shaking the very foundation of her life. For years she'd wondered what could have been if that motorcycle hadn't hit a patch of water and hydroplaned. Although a relationship begun so young had the cards stacked against it, maybe she and Zeke would have made it to Mexico. She might never have moved to Dallas and started her business. But on the other hand, maybe she would have spent the years happily married, maybe even had children of her own by now....

Although she was glad Zeke was nowhere in sight when she left the store, Linda was doubly disturbed to see Grover's Springs' own man in blue inspecting her car. Dwight Doggett, the most underworked crime fighter in the state of Texas, had been the bane of her existence since he'd caught her wrapping a house in seventh grade.

"Oh, no," she muttered under her breath as she accelerated the pram. "What's that for?" she asked the policeman.

The cop looked up and his eyes widened joyfully. "Lindy Potter! I'd heard you'd come back to visit. It's just like old times!"

He nodded happily at the yellow slip of paper under Linda's windshield wiper. Clearly, having a shiny red sports car to give tickets to made the man ecstatic.

"You've got to be kidding!" Linda said.

The policeman's genial expression turned hard. "No, ma'am. You're parked in front of a fire hydrant."

Linda gazed toward the back of her car, where her fender was just barely aligned with a hydrant. "That?" Linda asked indignantly. "Why, I missed it by a mile!"

Dwight Doggett returned his ballpoint pen to his pocket protector and laughed aloud, shaking his head. "It sure is great to have you around again, Lindy. It's plumb demoralizing around this old burg without you to keep me on my toes." He was still chuckling as he got back into his patrol car and eased down the street—probably to Murnet's Café to report this latest tidbit of news.

Linda plucked the ticket from her windshield. This was just her luck. She hadn't received a ticket since the last time she'd been in Grover's Springs. Something about this place brought out the devil in her—even when she was in park!

"Are you going to jail, Aunt Lindy?" one of the twins asked as she stuffed the baby into the car seat in the back of the sports car. Now she could understand why all those people drove minivans.

"I hope not," Linda said. Although, who could say for sure? It was still early in the day.

Despite the heat, she found herself hesitating before she turned on the ignition.

"Looks like you need a cupcake," the twin in the front seat said. Seth, she thought.

A cupcake? Instinctively Linda knew the kind the boy was referring to—the cream-filled, iced-chocolate cupcakes with the white squiggle down the top. She hadn't had one of those in years.

"I think you mean *you* want a cupcake, right?" she asked, unable to hold back a smile.

The kid shrugged. "Maybe."

"We'll see when we're at the store," Linda said, turning over the engine. Cupcakes would be easy to serve, at least. Cooking, aside from microwaving frozen dinners, was not her forte.

All the way through her trip to the store and the ensuing ride home, Linda attempted to focus her energy on the twins. Most of all, she tried not to think of Zeke and that kiss. Or his bitterness. Or her stubbornness. Or how much she wished her own problems could be solved by a healthy injection of sugary food....

Chapter Three

Linda sat on the lowest basement step, one hand holding a cream-filled cupcake, her other clutching the beeper at her hip—her one connection to the world of sanity. Her feet were soaking in a half foot of water as she watched her practically naked nephews frolic in the flooded room. At the top of the stairs, Emily lay in her crib, fussing at the ruckus her brothers were making. Oh, well. Hadn't Jane instructed her to use indulgence?

As she took a bite out of the cupcake, her taste buds perked up happily, and she looked down in amazement at the processed pastry. Now that she thought about it, these things had been her favorite when she was a kid, too. Maybe the preference was genetic. For the kids' sakes, she hoped lack of sense wasn't.

What on earth had made her think that she could fix a washing machine? She'd been too proud, or too cowardly, to let Zeke Howell into her house to check the thing out, and now she would have to go crawling back to him, anyway. Or live on top of a lake.

Finally she hit the creamy filling and her lips turned up in a smile. Zeke. He was a problem, all right. Six feet of sculpted muscle and trouble. What was he doing here?

Way back when, he had been as eager as she to get out of Grover's Springs, and with more reason. His father, apart from being a lousy provider, popped up only occasionally in Zeke's life, and then usually humiliated his son and wife by getting thrown in jail for drunkenness or misconduct.

His mother died of cancer before Zeke finished school, so George Warren had been the most consistent adult figure in Zeke's life. He had given him an after-school job, a meal when Zeke needed it and had been Zeke's personal cheering section at the high school graduation. Apart from Linda.

She'd met Zeke as a rebellious teen herself. Also motherless since the age of eight, she grew restless under the thumb of her stern minister father after Naomi left for college. Oh, she never did anything criminal or even especially dangerous, but somehow she managed to keep herself in enough trouble so that her father never was at peace.

Then she caught Zeke's eye one day at the E-Z Freeze, a teen hangout down by the interstate. With his motorcycle, strong jaw and defiant look in his eye, he was the closest thing to Marlon Brando that Grover's Springs had to offer her. And she took it.

During the next year she learned that the motorcycle wasn't so much a status symbol as it was the cheapest means of transportation Zeke could afford. And also that Zeke's defiant gaze held back a flood tide of hurt, concerning the hand life had dealt him. He lived to escape this small town, just as she did, and in this they found a bond as deep as any she'd discovered before or since.

She remembered one of Zeke's favorite pastimes, the "what if" game. He loved to imagine what life in Grover's Springs would have been like if things had been different. It could go on for hours. What if Vera Huckabee had looked like Lana Turner? What if his mother hadn't died? What if he had a million dollars?

Back in those days, the trivial had mixed well with the tragic, but now Linda could see only poignancy in their naiveté. They'd imagined themselves together forever. She especially remembered Zeke's favorite idle speculation—what if he could fix up the old place? The house where he and his father had lived, close to the edge of town, had been deteriorating back then. Zeke used to envision putting in decks and crazy turrets and knocking out walls that even then were on the verge of collapsing, anyway.

By now, Linda imagined, the Howell place had probably been leveled. *Oh, Zeke. What made you come back?*

Seeing him again had opened the gate to her memory that she had kept so carefully shut for so long. Occasionally over the past thirteen years she had allowed herself to think of Zeke. Who didn't think about her first love?

Yet she never examined too hard the fact that she wasn't able to commit to a long-term relationship with any of the men she'd dated since Zeke. And if she had thought about it, she probably would have said that On the Wing took priority in her life. But now...now even Jane didn't seem to think they would miss her. Her

fledgling business was flying on its own, which made
Linda feel anxious and vulnerable.

Every shred of common sense she possessed shouted
that she shouldn't see Zeke again. On the other hand,
she reminded herself impishly, Grover's Springs was
such a small town. How could she avoid him?

From the TV in the living room, the theme from
"Sesame Street" was blaring, and the twins were singing and splashing along. The words "Everything's
A-OK" struck Linda as being particularly funny, given
her circumstances. She had a basement full of water and
a weakness for the town handyman. Something about
that equation pointed to a solution, but all Linda could
think to do was let out another laugh and kick lightly at
a wave lapping at her ankle.

One of the twins saw her laughing and hollered,
"Come and play, Aunt Crazy!" His words echoed those
of the song—a song with a seductive, bubbly beat.

For one awkward split second, Linda actually hesitated.

Moments later, she was dancing in ring-around-the-
rosy fashion with the twins. Saul and Seth were singing,
but since Linda didn't remember all the words, she could
only hum along until they got to the refrain, which she
changed to "Can you tell me how to get, how to get to
Sycamore Street?" Her substitution brought peals of
laughter from the twins, and she herself threw back her
head and let out a long, pent-up whoop that seemed to
release every ounce of tension from her body.

How long had it been since she had laughed, really
laughed? Or danced or played? It felt so good, so freeing. She could remember feeling like this, often in fact.
It was a part of her personality that had shut down in
pursuit of a career and success. But as she pranced in the

slushy water, getting wetter by the second, she realized how much she missed this side of herself. Linda picked up one twin and then the other and spun them around. Her breath was coming in ragged gasps now, but for the life of her she couldn't stop spinning.

Lindy Potter had gone bug crazy. It did Zeke's heart good to see it.

The spectacle in Naomi Ward's basement amazed him. The three of them were laughing and singing, the TV in the living room was ear-splittingly loud, water was everywhere. Lindy had a look of pure glee on her face as she hurled her nephews around. Never in his thirty-one years of living had Zeke seen a sight that made him want to laugh as outrageously as he wanted to at this moment. This was the Lindy Potter he remembered.

Still, she wasn't going to like the fact that he of all people was witnessing this frivolous display. A wide smile still on his face, he raised his voice and asked, "Lindy?"

Linda froze. Slowly she lowered the twin in her arms to the ground and turned, dreading meeting the gaze that was surely going to have "I told you so" written all over it. Even the twins shuffled their feet in the murky water, obviously aware that things had gotten completely out of hand.

With as much confidence as she could muster in her sodden clothes, Linda lifted her chin and faced him. "I changed the pipes."

Seconds passed in which Zeke said nothing—just rubbed his jaw and looked back and forth between the floor, the shirtless twins and her own bedraggled self. She felt foolish, standing there in her soaking wet jeans, which were soggy and stiff against her legs. Foolish and exposed.

"Finally," he said at last, "a Lindy Potter I recognize."

The blood drained from Linda's face. "I know this looks stupid—"

"It looks great," Zeke interrupted. "Makes me want to take off my shirt and join you."

"Don't you dare!" Linda sassed back. "What on earth are you doing here, Zeke?"

"I rang the doorbell, although nobody heard me." He reached into the crib and picked up Emily, whose fussing immediately sputtered into intermittent hiccoughs. Looking back up at Linda, he asked, "Is the water off?"

Linda nodded and sloshed over to take Emily from him. "I think something's clogged."

Zeke sent her a look that said "No kidding" before plunging into the water to take a look around.

"Why don't you boys go clean up and watch the end of your program?" Linda suggested to the twins.

They slogged past her and climbed the steps, dripping all the way. More than the basement would need cleaning before this day was over, Linda noted ruefully, as she followed the twins upstairs and put the quieted baby back in her crib.

Already Zeke had zeroed in on the room's central drain, and the silence in the room, apart from the lapping of the water, made her nervous.

"Do you want to talk about it?" he asked in a wry, mocking voice, his eyes glinting with humor.

Linda grimaced. "I just ate a cupcake and the sugar went to my head."

He came up beside her on the steps, close. "Nice head," he commented, reaching out to push a stray damp lock of hair from her forehead. "Nice hair."

She ducked around the crib, positioning it between them. "I don't think you should have come here, Zeke."

He crossed his arms and regarded her seriously. With a nod toward her oceanic floor, he said, "Looks like you need me here. I thought you might."

Linda's chin jutted upward. "I'm sure I could figure this out...."

Zeke smiled again. "Why would you want to handle this yourself when I can fix it with less hassle?"

"I'm used to doing things myself."

"I hear you own your own business," Zeke said. "As boss, aren't you supposed to delegate?"

When he put it that way, Linda saw she was being foolish. He wanted to help her—and it couldn't have been any easier for him to come here than it would have been for her to call him.

A little buzz of anticipation zipped through her. Why not surrender the fight? She hadn't seen the man in thirteen years; being around him for an hour would be like putting balm to an itch. Besides, this was business. Just business.

"You're right," she said, finding it surprisingly simple to give in gracefully. She gestured across the room. "Fix away."

His eyebrows rose in curiosity. "Just like that?"

"We businesswomen are used to making snap decisions. Just tell me how much I owe you."

"Nothing," he said abruptly.

Linda threw up her hands in dismay. "I have to pay you, Zeke! Otherwise, it's no dice."

He leaned his weight on the crib and thought for a moment. "Okay," he said slowly, "if I let you pay me, it's a deal?"

"Absolutely."

"Shake on it," he said.

Linda looked down at the bronzed, sturdy hand extending toward her over the baby. She remembered that hand, remembered the magic it could work as it caressed the length of her back, and the havoc it could wreak on her senses. Seemingly without permission, her own smaller hand reached across until, centimeters away, she could feel the heat of his skin like an electrical current drawing her hand forward.

Linda closed her eyes, swallowed hard and shook.

"Dinner," he said.

Her eyelids popped open. She'd been duped! "That's not fair," she said, retrieving her hand immediately.

"Why? It'll probably come out cheaper than the hourly rate."

Just then, Linda looked down at Emily and remembered—the children. God bless them. "It's impossible," she explained. "I can't go out while I've got the kids."

"Oh, right. I forgot that they don't allow children in public these days," Zeke quipped. "But I meant having dinner at home, anyway."

"Oh." Linda shook her head. The cagey devil had her cornered. She pulled out her last defense. "It won't be very appetizing. I'm a bad cook, anyway, and because I'm trying to be a good aunt, I let Saul and Seth pick out the groceries."

A wide smile of triumph lighted up Zeke's face. "Then I guess we won't be having brussels sprouts."

"No, we're safe from that, at least."

But as they set about draining the basement side by side, safe was the last thing Linda felt. At first she hung around the periphery of the room, staying as far away from Zeke as she could possibly manage. As she retrieved floating objects and took them to higher ground, Zeke worked on unclogging the drain. Both showed no outward sign of marking the other's whereabouts, but Linda seemed instinctively to sense Zeke's every movement.

After five minutes of that, he looked up abruptly. "Hey."

Linda's pulse sped as they made eye contact. "What?" His voice had a huskier timbre than before, and his eyes regarded her more softly.

"I was thinking . . ."

Linda swallowed. "Yes?"

A reassuring smile touched his lips. "What if all the stray dogs in Grover's Springs formed a commune?"

Linda's heart tripped twice, and she folded her arms across her stomach to steady herself.

"I'd better start dinner."

Fish fingers. Now those were a blast from her past.

Linda pushed the lukewarm battered rectangle around her plate, toward her macaroni and cheese. She thought suddenly of her sister's perfect size-six figure. How did Naomi maintain it? She herself was at least a size larger, and she didn't have to consume a steady diet of grease and cheese and peanut butter. Except for this week . . .

Nevertheless, she had to admit this stuff was kind of tasty. Maybe the microwave dinners she lived on really weren't very good. Or maybe this food just gave her that warm, fuzzy feeling of being a kid again. Although when she looked over at Saul and Seth, they didn't seem too interested in dinner. Something was up with those two. Every once in a while they would throw each other covert glances that seemed calculated to make her nervous.

They were also making pathetic little whimpering sounds that didn't even sound human.

And, of course, added to this was the green-eyed man sitting across the table from her. Zeke had said little up till now, but his gaze had been focused on her. The only way she could escape it was by looking down at her plate, but even then, she could feel him watching her.

"Aunt Lindy plays with her food," Seth observed.

Linda's head snapped up.

"It's not polite to play with your food," his brother put in.

Her fork clattered against her plate. Had she been playing with her food? The smile on Zeke's face said that she had, and his next words confirmed it.

"Is that a castle you're making out of your macaroni and cheese?"

She looked down at her plate as the blood rushed to her face. Just as he had said, her food was piled up in a rather juvenile clump of mounds. Had she really done that?

"Looks like a mountain!"

It did at that, Linda thought critically. More specifically, it looked like the only kind of mountain the twins would have ever seen—the ones in Dr. Seuss books.

"Or a kitten," Seth said. "Aunt Lindy, me and Saul found a kitten."

"Oh, really?" Linda said, wondering whether Naomi would want her to correct their grammar. Knowing Naomi, she would.

"I didn't know you had an artistic streak," Zeke said, sending a quick wink across the table.

Linda laughed. "Neither did I. Maybe all this new diet has brought out a latent talent."

For a moment, she allowed herself the luxury of basking in Zeke's gaze. She'd forgotten how intense it was, how much he could reveal—and hold back. He'd told her very little about himself today.

"We found him in the backyard."

Linda smiled benignly at the chubby-cheeked twin who'd spoken, unable to remember what the child was referring to. Just as quickly, the boy's attention was diverted to his napkin, which he appeared to be making into different shapes.

"Where have you been all these years, Zeke?" Linda asked, in hopes that she could keep up better with the adult at the table.

He thought for a moment. "Around."

"That's specific," Linda joked. "Around the world?"

"Well, this part of it." He looked directly in her eyes. "I went to Mexico right off."

Linda felt her face redden. "What happened?"

Zeke smiled a lazy smile and stretched his legs out under the table. "You know, it's a funny thing. All those years ago we kind of forgot about something."

"What was that?"

"Money." He laughed. "I ran out of it in about a month. So I went up to California and did seasonal jobs on the farms up there. After a while I figured I could make more money on repair work, like I always did for George. I crossed this whole country, fixing it as I went."

Linda laughed with him. "Did you make it all the way on a motorcycle, like you always said you would?"

"Partway, I did," Zeke said. "After a second accident in Iowa, I wised up and invested in a truck."

"It doesn't sound as romantic as you'd hoped," Linda said a little sadly. Their eyes met for a long moment across the table.

"It was lonelier," he said in a low voice.

"You wanna see it?"

Linda broke her gaze from Zeke and looked at the twins. See it? What were they talking about?

"'Cause if you do, we've got him right here."

"Who—"

Before she could spit out the question, it was answered as a perfect yellow fuzzball appeared on the table, no bigger in size than her cupped hands. Pale blue eyes stared unblinkingly up at her so innocently that any thoughts of objection completely eluded her mind—especially when the tiny creature let out a soft cooing meow.

"A kitten!" Linda cooed back, unable to keep the squeakiness out of her voice. "You're so cuuuuute!" She'd always had a notorious soft spot for animals, and though her father had never officially allowed them, she was always taking in strays. It was one thing she'd missed in her years as an apartment dweller.

"His name's Hippopotamus," Seth said, getting the word out with surprising ease.

"That's a big name for such a little kitty," Linda said, and the twins nodded proudly. "May I hold Hippo?"

"Hippolomatus," Saul corrected.

"He wants some macaroni and cheese," said his brother.

"I think we can rustle him up some tuna fish, at least," Linda said. Slowly she reached forward to pet the kitten, who was warming to all this attention like a trouper. Linda stroked the crown of the kitten's head with her index finger, and the little animal immediately started purring at a volume all out of proportion to his size. His loudness elicited a tentative giggle from Linda. She didn't want to startle him.

"Where did you find him?" she asked the twins.

"Outside," they said, curious that she would ask a question they'd already explained for her.

"In the yard?" When she looked over, both boys were nodding.

Dumped. She remembered acquiring her pets as a child in a similar fashion. People with baby animals targeted the families in town with children. It was a foolhardy, reckless strategy that luckily often worked, especially on bleeding hearts like herself.

"Can we keep him, Aunt Lindy?"

"Well, I don't see why no—"

Zeke cleared his throat. Loudly. Startled, she looked up to see him slowly shaking his head. She looked back down at the kitten. How could they not keep something so adorable!

Yet in the back of her mind she heard a warning bell—and Jane's husky voice saying the word *firm*.

"Mommy wouldn't let us have a puppy."

The muted sound of warning bells rose to a full four-alarm siren. *Mommy*. Naomi. Naomi, who had grown up grumbling about litter boxes and slobbery mutts. Her sister had never been wild about animals, to say the least.

Partial damage had already been done, Linda realized as she noted the desperation in her nephews' eyes. Hippopotamus, it was clear, already belonged to them. How could she tell them otherwise?

She inhaled deeply and took the only course she could think of at the moment, which was simply to pass the buck. "We'll have to ask your mother."

"But she didn't let us keep that puppy!" Seth objected. His brother answered by turning beet red and immediately beginning to gush.

"I wanna keep it!" Seth yelled above his brother's sobs.

Confronted with such anger, and with her own mixed feelings, Linda drew a blank. Frustration welled. If they hadn't said that about the puppy, she would be tempted to throw caution to the wind and give them permission, and persuade Naomi later. But she couldn't set the kids up for heartbreak.

She looked back at the kitten, and then, in desperation, to Zeke. His expression was sympathetic and as frankly torn as she was sure her own was. Finally he leaned forward and put an arm around Saul's shoulder.

"Hey," he said. "Lindy didn't say you *couldn't* keep Hippopotamus, you know."

"Mommy'll make us give him back," Seth said belligerently.

"Not necessarily," Zeke said. His words surprised Linda.

"How's that?" Seth asked, echoing her own thoughts exactly. Saul swallowed a sob and looked curiously into Zeke's face.

"Well..." Zeke rubbed his jaw with his free hand. "One thing you could do is let your mom know what a good pet Hippopotamus is by showing that he won't be any trouble. And that means that you have to show that you can take care of him really well. Especially while your aunt's here. Can you do that?"

The boys nodded vigorously and Zeke stood.

"Then why don't we find a place where you can keep Hippopotamus. How about the screened porch out back?"

"Yeah!" they cried.

For the next thirty minutes, the four of them scurried around finding ways to maximize the comfort level of Hippo's stay on the screened back porch. For a bed, the boys found an old shirt in the pile Naomi put aside for dusting rags, and Linda made a makeshift litter box from a used aluminum roasting pan, which looked like the Grand Canyon next to that kitten.

"I hope this works," Linda said when Zeke followed her into the kitchen after leaving the boys with their new friend.

"What else could you do?"

"That's the terrible part," Linda lamented. "*You* were the one who remained levelheaded. I was petrified."

He laughed. "You did look kind of nervous."

"Kind of? You would have thought I'd been confronted by a lion in the Serengeti rather than a kitten on the dinner table. But he was so cute!"

Zeke hesitated, a smile pulling at his lips as he rubbed his jaw. "That's another item you might want to leave for Naomi."

Puzzled, Linda looked up. "What's that?"

"Explaining to those kids that Hippopotamus is a girl kitty."

"Oh." She hadn't even thought of that. Zeke probably thought her a complete fool, first squealing like an idiot over the fuzzy little animal, and then being unable to deal with her nephews. "I probably could have handled it if I'd had some warning," she explained in her defense as she loaded dinner dishes into the dishwasher. "It was just so sudden!"

Zeke crossed his arms. "Admit it," he teased, "you just don't like to say no."

She smiled back saucily. "Not when faced with a hunka-hunka purring fuzz."

Was she actually flirting with Zeke? she wondered suddenly. That wasn't a good idea, no matter how nice he'd been about the kids. This was the man who had broken her heart, she reminded herself sternly. She felt warmth creep up her neck and she turned back to her work. Work had always been her refuge, she realized as she scanned the kitchen for any stray dinnerware.

Unfortunately, when she felt a slight but insistent tug on her shorts, she knew she couldn't hide for long.

"We wanna story."

"You do?" Linda bent toward them as she wiped her hands on a cup towel. "Then why don't you go read one of those books I saw on the shelves in your room?"

The two sets of eyes blinked at her. They still seemed to be waiting for something.

"And get ready for bed," she said, feeling a tug on her sleeve. She darted a glance toward Zeke, who was sending her a curious look. What was this, pull-on-Linda day? "I'll be up in a moment to say good-night," she promised.

"Earth to Lindy."

She threw up her hands. "For heaven's sakes, what is it?" She turned on Zeke, losing patience.

He leaned in and whispered, for her ears alone, "Could you read when you were four?"

"What do you—" Words stopped as understanding dawned. She looked down at the twins again, feeling like a complete idiot.

"We want you to make us a story," Seth said.

"Those are the best kind," Saul agreed.

Panic surged through Linda. Make up a story? The twins' plaintive eyes tore at her, but butterflies flopped in her stomach, as if she had accidentally stepped on-stage at the Metropolitan Opera and now had to come up with an off-the-cuff aria.

She swallowed. She sweated. She opened her mouth to speak and nothing came out.

"Tell you what, fellas," she heard Zeke say. She looked over to see him leading them out of the room. "*I'll* tell you a story."

"Yea!"

"You can't do that," Linda said.

The three of them turned to look back at her. Zeke's eyebrows rose expectantly. "Sure I can," he said. "Working in people's houses during the day you end up talking more to the kids than to the actual clients."

She had meant that she thought it was time for him to go home, but apparently, Zeke was determined to stay. And the kids certainly wanted him to. *Face it,* a little inner voice cajoled, *you want him to, too.*

The story began in the usual once-upon-a-time way, but after that it was a crap shoot. The world Zeke wove was filled with greedy buzzards, cigar-smoking bears, a beaver named Chip who was born to ramble, and a seductive lady parrot named Maud, who Linda suspected with a faint twinge of jealousy to be based on someone in real life.

It was a far cry from the Three Little Pigs, but Linda found herself becoming engrossed in the tale all the same. She worried whether such a seamy story was quite appropriate, but the shady deals of the bear and the buzzard fascinated the twins, and she supposed the story was redeemed somewhat by Chip the Beaver's industriousness always foiling them in the end. Maud, on the other hand, was an entirely different matter....

Linda suspected Zeke was putting in the racier aspects of the story to hold the attention of the grown-ups in the room. Not that she needed a lusty parrot to keep her awake. She was too focused on the storyteller, and anxious about what she was going to do once the story was over. Considering the reckless way she was beginning to feel inside, she needed to get the man out of her house. Fast.

"Lindy?" Zeke tried to get her attention.

The dimly lit room was suddenly very quiet, except for the soft snores coming from the twins. Startled, she looked up.

"They just dropped off," he said in a low whisper, then smiled. "Looks like I nearly put you to sleep, too."

"Hardly," Linda replied. "Your bedtime story packed as much punch as a Warner Brothers melodrama."

They got up and turned out the remaining light, then silently walked out of the room. What now? Zeke wondered. He could sense that Linda was ready for him to leave, but that was the last thing he wanted to do as he followed her along the landing.

He'd kissed her once today, on a whim. But it had stuck with him, just as memories of Lindy had stuck with him all these years. And the moment he'd seen her dancing with those kids in that water—well, it was as if he'd gotten his best friend back.

"Lindy."

When he whispered her name, she stopped so abruptly that he almost bumped into her back. He grabbed her shoulders to steady himself, although once steadied, he couldn't let go. Her gray eyes were even softer in the muted light. They were only on the second-story landing of Naomi Ward's house, but to Zeke, the air seemed suddenly thinner. He needed more than just oxygen.

"Zeke, we need . . ."

As he pulled her closer, her breath caught. One of her hands held on to his arm, but the other kept a white-knuckled grip on the banister. She was torn, like him. Zeke knew rekindling was probably a bad idea in this instance. If Lindy had wanted him, she could have had him thirteen years ago—and every day since.

Nevertheless, when their lips met, he felt as if he might melt with the relief that soft pressure brought. He gathered her closer, wishing he could somehow meld the past and present. They were adults now, but they had adult obstacles, too. Yet . . . what if they could start over, he thought, what if . . .

"Zeke," Linda said, dragging her lips away from his.

Linda tried to straighten out her thoughts as she set her blouse to rights. Falling for Zeke Howell again wasn't just a bad idea, it was potentially disastrous. The only reason she was even vulnerable to such a thing was because she was stuck alone in Grover's Springs, and the man happened to be good with children. And houses. And her.

But no more. She had her life back in Dallas to consider, and her business. She couldn't throw caution to the wind after all these years of carefully avoiding ending up the broken-hearted shell Zeke had left her at seventeen.

"We need to talk," she announced firmly.

"Uh-oh."

Zeke knew what was coming. Although Linda remained mute as she turned and marched down the stairs, he could clearly hear her voice saying phrases like "lost our heads" and "will not be repeated" in his mind. The militaristic set of her shoulders was telegraphing the message "never again." His heart sank.

And then, suddenly, the world turned upside down. Literally. One moment Linda was striding defiantly down the steps in front of him, and in the next her arms were making frantic loopy circles in a hopeless attempt to catch her balance.

"Lindy!"

Too late his arm shot out to catch her. Lindy soared through the air, taking the old oak banister with her.

Chapter Four

Linda reclined in a sea of chintz on Naomi's couch, her leg elevated dramatically on a three-tiered pillow mound that Zeke had fashioned for her. Her sprained ankle throbbed, but aside from not being able to walk very well, and a few other aches and pains from her ski jump off the staircase—a fall resulting from a stray shiny red toy car—she felt fine. Foolish, but fine.

So fine that two hours of sitting on the couch watching mindless morning television became too much for her. With Zeke in the hallway repairing the banister and entertaining the kids, except for Emily, who was asleep in a playpen set up in the living room, Linda was left with nothing to occupy her mind except thinking about him and his sudden reappearance in her life.

She tried turning her mind to business. Yesterday, Jane had made it sound as though the place was doing just fine without her. How could that be? Usually a million troublesome little problems cropped up every single day—anything from complaints from major accounts to troubles ordering new window cleaner.

If she didn't call Jane, she was certain to end up like one of those poor guests on those syndicated talk shows. "Next up... She thought she'd sprained her ankle, but really she'd lost her mind!"

Zeke had made her promise not to walk on the leg, but the phone was all the way across the room. After a furtive glance toward the hallway where he was working, she gritted her teeth and swung her leg over the end of the couch. Then, ignoring the violent throbbing in her right ankle, she quickly pushed herself off the couch and began a mad hop-dash across the room to retrieve the clunky black phone that had to be as old as she was.

By the time she made it back to the couch, she was perspiring from the shooting pain in her leg, but triumphant. With another glance toward the hallway, she dialed her office. Jane picked up after half a ring.

"Jane, it's me."

"Is something wrong? Why are you whispering?" Jane whispered, too.

"I've sprained my ankle." After a puzzled silence from her employee, Linda launched into a more detailed explanation of her domestic calamity.

"I get it," Jane said dryly, "you're whispering so that the love of your life won't realize you've become one of those businesswomen types who can't be away from the office a single day without going nuts."

There was so much to object to in what her friend had just said Linda hardly knew where to begin. "Zeke is not the love of my life," she blurted in a vehement, barely audible tone.

"Okay, correction. The hunk of your life."

Unfortunately Linda feared that was the case. She'd never met another man who attracted her like Zeke, and probably never would. "Anyway, I am not a hysterical businesswoman."

"That's good."

Linda froze. "Why?" she barked. "Is something wrong? Oh, I knew I should have told Naomi I couldn't be away from the office for so long!"

"Linda, calm down. Absolutely nothing is happening here. Nothing but the sounds of phones ringing and money being made."

Slowly Linda's pulse returned to normal. "Jane, you shouldn't scare me like that."

Jane laughed. "I just said that it was a good thing you're not a hysterical businesswoman."

"Okay, so maybe I'm a little paranoid when it comes to On the Wing."

"But enough about this boring place," Jane said. "Tell me more about your ankle. Better yet, tell me more about the hunk."

As if he'd heard his cue, Zeke peered around the living room entrance. When he caught sight of the phone, its long cord stretching across the room in a telltale sign of Linda having disobeyed his orders, a frown furrowed his brow. Reluctantly he ducked back out of sight to give her privacy.

Since there was no longer any need to whisper, Linda said in a normal voice, "Jane, it pains me to hear you call my life's work 'this boring place.'"

"The hunk's listening in, isn't he?"

"His name is Zeke," Linda whispered, cupping her mouth with her hand as she spoke, "and I simply feel it's silly to whisper in my own home."

"You obviously didn't grow up with seven brothers and sisters. If everyone didn't whisper, the place would've sounded like Grand Central. And speaking of my family, are you sure your ankle's okay? I could call my sister Frieda."

"Is she a doctor?" Linda asked.

"No, but she played basketball. She was always spraining something—I'm sure she'd know what to do."

"That's okay. Zeke seems to know what to do, too."

"Mmm," Jane agreed. "And he's probably a lot better looking than Frieda."

Linda conjured up memories from the night before. It had taken her long minutes to convince Zeke that she hadn't broken anything and didn't need an ambulance. Finally, he'd gathered her in his arms and swept her into the next room. She knew it was foolish to romanticize gallantry that stemmed from necessity. After all, she'd just taken a whopping, pathetically clutzy fall. But even so, in his arms she'd felt light, not awkward, beautiful instead of disheveled and . . .

Which only proved that her imagination had survived the fall quite well, while her good sense seemed to have gone out the window!

"Please don't forget to beep me if anything comes along that needs my attention," she instructed.

"I doubt that will happen. Just relax for a week," Jane told her. "It's allowed. You're the boss."

After she had hung up the phone, Linda closed her eyes and rested against the pillows for a moment. Yes, relax. She could do that for one week, couldn't she? The business didn't require her presence twenty-four hours a day, three hundred and sixty-five days a year.

Someone giggled. Linda's eyes snapped open and scoped the room. Suddenly two heads popped up from behind the couch.

"You weren't asleep!" one of the twins said. Seth.

"Have you seen *Sleeping Beauty,* Aunt Lindy?"

Linda smiled. "Not in a long, long time."

"We was going to pretend like you were the girl in the movie."

"'Cause you were asleep."

"And Hippolomatus was gonna be the prince." The cat was promptly plopped on the backrest of the couch. She meowed affably.

"Kissing's gross but he doesn't mind."

"And we couldn't think of another prince."

"Zeke could be a prince!" Saul exclaimed.

Hearing his name, Zeke ambled into the doorway and leaned against the frame just in time to see Linda's face turn beet red.

Seth frowned at his brother. "Zeke doesn't want to kiss Aunt Linda!"

Lacking the courage to even see how Zeke was reacting to all of this, Linda snatched up the kitten and gave it a big kiss on its tiny triangular nose. "There, see? I'm awake."

"You'd be even more awake if Zeke kissed you," Saul said earnestly.

Linda couldn't have agreed more. She handed back the alarmed kitten in silence.

"Can we keep Hippo, Aunt Lindy?" Seth's big blue eyes stared pleadingly at her. "Can't you tell Mama we can keep him?"

"Please?" Saul echoed. "You kissed him. You must like him."

Linda stared, dumbfounded. Hadn't this already been settled? She tried to remember exactly what Zeke had told them last night.

"Hey, now, fellas," Zeke interrupted. "We don't want to disturb your aunt too much. Why don't you take Hippo out back?"

Seth's chin jutted out willfully at Zeke, but after a short staredown, he gave in and turned to his brother. "C'mon," he said reluctantly, shaking his red head. As they trudged away, Zeke strolled by Emily's playpen to check on the progress of her sleeping.

"I forgot how children are," Linda said, filling the silence. "Tenacious. Energetic. You really do know a lot about kids, for never having had any." A disturbing thought occurred to her. "I mean...you haven't had any, have you?"

"No," Zeke said. Suddenly he was frowning, too. "You?"

"No."

They stared at each other for a moment, smiling again. Linda didn't know why she felt a sense of relief to know he hadn't had a child with another woman. She just did. But maybe that was selfish.

"I don't want to pry..."

Zeke shot her a winning grin. "Don't you? I do."

Linda laughed. "Okay, me first. I'm surprised you decided to settle here, Zeke."

"Nothing's settled," he corrected. He thought briefly about George and that store. He would never have dreamed that he'd end up a storekeeper. Never in his wildest dreams.

Of course, his wildest dreams had always been about the woman in front of him. Wild and Crazy Lindy. Only now she was different, too. Anyone who saw her reclining on the sofa in a long, silky scoop-necked shirt the color of spun gold would agree. The shirt was worn lazily over white stretch pants, and two shiny gold flats were strewn at the foot of the couch. Lindy had done pretty well for herself, and she looked comfortable in her success.

What must she think of him? he wondered suddenly. He'd never stopped to consider that she might simply think him a throwback from her youth. A hick. Not only that, a woman like Lindy probably had someone waiting for her in Dallas. Someone more like herself.

Linda looked up at him curiously, fingering one of the chunky earrings she was wearing. Something had brought their conversation to a grinding halt. "What are you thinking?"

Zeke tried to keep his expression a blank. "Just that I should get back to work. Sorry, I guess I don't have time to be curious."

Through the rest of the day, he worked on the banister as if by rote, going through the motions like a zombie. Every once in a while he would snap out of it. Unfortunately, it was usually because he found himself needing to see Lindy again. Or he'd hear her calling that damned office of hers, as if she were hoping for trouble. So he'd trot off to the kitchen to make her a cup of tea, or bring her a snack. And of course he had to make lunch for her and the twins.

Each break—each time he got to have just another look at her pretty face, the face he'd dreamed of for so long—would fuel him for another forty-five minutes to an hour of work. Then he'd be back, bringing her a soda, changing the baby's diaper for her, asking if he could fetch her anything. He was never going to finish

that banister. Just like he was never going to escape
Lindy's spell.

Finally he knocked off and fixed dinner. He couldn't
just leave her to shift for herself, could he?

As they sat at a table on the screened back porch, the
balmy June night bright around them, Linda was grateful Zeke had stayed. She knew every hour his truck remained parked in front of her house meant gossip, but
would Mrs. Huckabee have helped her with the kids or
have made her this yummy dinner—and most important, would Mrs. Huckabee have thought to have the
kids decorate their hot dog buns with mustard smiley
faces and ketchup mustaches?

Zeke was a natural, Linda ruminated as she munched
down her frank. She hadn't eaten a hot dog in ages, and
it tasted surprisingly good. Just like all the little snacks
he'd brought her throughout the day. There was something seductive in having a man wait on her, hand and
sprained foot. Zeke's tender ministrations had succeeded where Jane's soothing words had failed. Linda
felt—finally—relaxed.

In fact, listening to the cicadas drone lazily on,
watching Zeke and the kids laughing, and feeling Emily
gently beating her tiny baby fists against her leg as she
held her, Linda felt as though she were in a dream. As if
she'd bumped her head in her fall down the stairs and
woken up with a family of her own.

She sucked in a short, choked breath, suddenly hit by
a wave of what-ifs. If things had turned out differently,
she and Zeke could have married and settled into this,
her old family house, or even his, although that place
was probably long gone by now. They could even have
had three kids in that amount of time…he was so good
with kids. He must want some of his own someday.

Just then, Zeke shot her a concerned stare. "Are you okay?"

Linda snapped back to reality. "What?"

"You looked kind of dazed. For a second there I thought you might pass out."

Linda worried momentarily that he could have read her fanciful thoughts. But, thank goodness, he couldn't. Thoughts of marriage and children were fine as idle speculation—she certainly wanted both those things sometime in the future. When she wasn't so busy. Zeke had simply seduced her with his man-about-the-house routine. When she woke up tomorrow, she would still be a woman with a business to run.

The important thing was not to do anything rash—like kiss Zeke again. There was no sense in starting something that was bound to end unhappily. She was going to send Zeke home right after dinner tonight. And then she'd call Jane and talk to her about that property in Houston that she'd been thinking about leasing.

"I guess I did feel a little dazed," she said. "But I'm back on planet Earth now." She hoped.

Zeke whammed the hammer directly onto his thumb and bit back a ferocious yowl of pain.

"I bet that hurt," Seth observed as Zeke flapped his hand back and forth through the air.

He nodded. You'd think he'd never hammered a nail before! And he should have had this job finished yesterday. The only reason he hadn't was because he was behaving like a fool and mooning over his girlfriend from more than ten years ago. It just didn't make sense. He'd left the Bledsoes with a half-finished roof just so he could do this favor for Linda. The Bledsoes, who had generously thrown a lot of work his way. Yet here it was, nearly noon on Wednesday, and here he was, on a staircase, not a roof.

Today Linda was hobbling around the house, which made it difficult for him to concentrate. Through the corner of his eye he would capture glimpses of her passing through a doorway or limping across the hall. Sometimes he would just hear her banging around her sister's kitchen, making a phone call, talking to the baby. It would have been less distracting if she'd plopped right down on a step and started gabbing at him.

For well over a decade he'd managed to keep that woman in perspective, but now their chance meeting had twisted him all out of kilter. He'd thought he was over her, over the bitterness, over his crazy attraction to her. The times in the past when he had thought of her, it was usually with stinging pride. He'd remember lying in a hospital bed, watching her walk silently out the door and feeling like she'd just kicked him in the teeth.

Sometimes he would think of how he'd picked her up early in the morning the day they'd started their journey, and how jubilant they'd been to finally be on their way. Then, slowly, he would live through the sensation of hitting a patch of water and having his bike, his girl, his dreams pulled out from under him.

No matter how wild and crazy Lindy Potter was reputed to have been, she hadn't been wild enough to defy her father and visit, or even call. That's when he had learned the real difference between them. "Good" folks like Linda could always get into little accidents and be sheltered from the consequences, whereas he was stuck wondering whether he'd lost Lindy forever *and* if he was going to be able to pay the hospital bill.

Afterward his blame had too often fallen on his old man, or Linda's father, and too seldom where it actually belonged—squarely on his own shoulders. He'd been a damn fool to run off with a girl like Linda in the first place. The son of the town drunk couldn't run off with a minister's daughter without expecting some kind of retribution.

Just then she clumped through the hallway on her way to the living room.

"Aunt Lindy! Zeke hurt his hand!"

Zeke let out an annoyed sigh and Linda stopped, frowning. "Are you okay?"

"Sure," Zeke said. The bite in his voice had nothing to do with his pulverized thumb and everything to do with thirteen years ago. He looked away and cursed silently when he heard her footsteps approaching him.

"Let me see," she said.

"It's okay," Zeke insisted.

"Zeke..."

To hear her say his name was irresistible, and almost out of instinct he looked up into her worried gray eyes. Slowly he offered his hand for her inspection, dreading and craving the moment of contact.

"There's nothing wrong that I can see." In contradiction to her words, her brows puckered even more.

Zeke smiled when she didn't let go of his hand. "Told you so."

She looked at him, alarmed, as if she'd been caught doing something illicit. His hand was promptly dropped. "I just wanted to make sure."

"And how are you doing?"

"You mean my foot?" She laughed. "I'm stumping around just fine. I bet by the weekend I'll be dancing in the streets again."

"In the streets, or in the Cornelius Grover fountain?"

Linda caught the mischievous gleam in his eye and returned it. "Come to think of it," she quipped, "some good old-fashioned hydrotherapy might be just the ticket."

"Might be," Zeke returned, reaching instinctively for her hand again. It felt right to see her like this, not on edge the way she sometimes was around him, or worrying about that travel agency she ran in Dallas. He remembered how much fun he used to have bantering with her, how easy she always was to talk to. Like their silly "what if" game...

The doorbell rang, startling them both.

"I'll get it!" Seth cried, and his brother echoed him. They charged down the steps much faster than Linda could hobble after them.

When Seth slowly swung the door open, revealing the pinched, bespectacled face of Mrs. Huckabee, Linda bit back a gasp—Vera Huckabee was the last person she'd expected to come calling.

Saul tugged on Linda's shirt. "That's the lady from next door," he said.

Linda twisted her mouth into a smile. "I know. Would you like to come in, Mrs. Huckabee?" Obviously she did, or she wouldn't have been standing there holding a foil-wrapped plate while they all gaped at her.

"I can only stay for a minute," she said as she sashayed through the door, handed the plate to Linda, and headed straight for the living room, peering curiously about the house on her way. The rest of them shuffled after her.

Mrs. Huckabee sat down on the edge of the couch, straight-backed with her hands folded on her knees, and surveyed the room carefully over the rims of her bifocals. "Lindy Potter," she mused in her unamused throaty voice. "You always were an odd girl."

Linda chuckled and ducked nervously into the chair next to the couch, feeling as awkward as she had when she was ten. For a moment they all watched as Mrs. Huckabee stared around the room, probably gathering fodder for the Sit-n-Chat gossip mill.

"I brought brownies," Mrs. Huckabee said, her gaze falling on Zeke, who was hanging back in the doorway. The twins stood by him. "Do you remember my brownies, Lindy?"

"Wow, do I," Linda said, suddenly remembering with mouth-watering clarity how delicious they were. She lifted the foil and removed one gooey, fudgie square.

"I brought them for the boys," Mrs. Huckabee said before Linda could get the brownie to her mouth.

"Oh, of course." Linda quickly replaced the brownie. "Guys, do you want some brownies?" The twins appeared beside her in a flash, and Linda carefully gave a brownie to each.

"And of course, Zeke should have one, too," Mrs. Huckabee said, turning to beam on Zeke, who smiled back. "I saw what a wonderful job you did on the banister."

"I had an accident on the stairs," Linda began to explain nervously.

"I heard all about it," Mrs. Huckabee interrupted. "Not to mention, George Warren explained to me about the other kind of accidents y'all have."

Zeke's smile disappeared until he bit into one of those heavenly brownies. "George has a big mouth."

"Dear George," Mrs. Huckabee said with a sigh. "He always speaks of you fondly. And of what a hard worker you are." The lady peeked around the back of the couch.

What was Mrs. Huckabee looking for? Linda wondered. Dust? She crossed her arms and sank back into her chair.

Mrs. Huckabee's lips turned into their usual frown as she focused on Linda again. "I certainly was surprised when I saw Naomi leaving these children with you."

Linda's teeth clenched. She'd been waiting for that comment, and she planned to let the woman know just how in control she was. "I've been having a marvelous time with my niece and nephews. Seth," she instructed, hoping she sounded motherly, "careful you don't drop crumbs on the carpet."

"That's Saul!" Seth corrected.

Linda squirmed in the silence that followed. Saul's next comment only made her sink lower into her chair.

"Aunt Lindy gave me and Seth a kitten!"

The elderly lady smiled happily down at the boy. "A kitten of your very own?" she asked. As Saul nodded enthusiastically, Mrs. Huckabee shot Linda a skeptical glance. "I didn't think Naomi liked animals, though you always did."

The woman was no doubt remembering the time when a Labrador Linda had taken in had dug up half her pansy beds trying to decide where to bury a bone. "Naomi will have to decide whether we keep the kitten, of course," she conceded.

"Well," Mrs. Huckabee said, tweaking each twin on his chocolate-stuffed cheek. "I'm sure if anyone can convince Naomi, it's you, Lindy. You always did run roughshod over everyone."

Suddenly, looking rejuvenated by about ten years, the elderly woman hopped off the couch. "It certainly is nice to see you two together again."

Linda and Zeke frowned in unison. "What?"

"It's like they were saying at the Sit-n-Chat when I was getting my hair done this morning." Vera patted her hair back primly. "First you were sweethearts in high school, and now...well, you know."

"Our being here together is just coincidence," Zeke defended. He didn't want it to get around that he was chasing after Lindy Potter again. Even if he was. Sort of.

"Yes, but I must say, from the looks of things..."

Linda smiled, both at Zeke's discomfort and Vera Huckabee's hasty assumption. "Yes, I suppose it does look funny."

"Yes," Mrs. Huckabee said. She looked from Linda to Zeke and back again. "Well?"

Linda sent Zeke a sly wink meant to stump poor Mrs. Huckabee. "I bet it looks like we've set up house here, almost." Vera nodded eagerly, and Linda covered a smile with her hand. "Well, not even almost. I suppose it just plain looks that way."

"Linda," Zeke said warningly.

"Oh, Zeke," Linda said, feeling reckless, "we've never been the kind of people who mind what other people think."

"Yeah, but—"

"Well!" Mrs. Huckabee exclaimed, heading for the door. "It's certainly been a pleasure, Lindy."

Zeke fumed as he watched Linda show Mrs. Huckabee out. What had just happened here? It was as though Lindy had knowingly misled Vera, playing up his attraction to her as if it were a joke.

"Can you believe her?" Linda asked when she stumped back in. She looked at the nearly empty brownie plate in front of the twins and bit back a laugh. Those kids were bottomless pits!

Zeke watched her toss her head carelessly as she flopped down onto the couch. She propped her weak ankle onto the coffee table. It was wrapped in an elastic bandage and looked almost comical with the wedge shoes she had on, but Zeke didn't smile.

"Why so glum, Zeke?" she asked.

Her breezy little voice annoyed him. Maybe it had taken Mrs. Huckabee's visit to get it through his thick skull. Linda didn't take him any more seriously now than she had thirteen years ago. He squared his shoulders, turned and left the room.

"Zeke?" Linda hollered after him. "What's wrong?"

"Don't worry your pretty head about it, Lindy."

She got up and followed him briskly to the kitchen. "What's the matter?" she asked. "What did I do?"

Zeke opened a cabinet, grabbed a glass and poured water from the tap. "I don't like being played for a fool, Lindy."

She stared at him, incredulous. "You mean what I did to Mrs. Huckabee? I thought you of all people would think it was amusing. She's such a snoop!"

"So you used me to mislead her," he accused. "And not just me, but the fact that we used to be a couple. I guess you think that's pretty funny."

Suddenly Linda felt about two inches tall. She hadn't thought of it that way. "I'm sorry," she said, meaning it.

Zeke downed the rest of his water with one gulp, then placed the glass in the sink. "You haven't changed, Lindy. You're still daddy's little girl, dallying with a boy from the wrong side of the tracks."

Angered, Linda put her hands on her hips. "That's not true and you know it!"

"All I know is that you used me once, Lindy. Then you walked away and left me feeling like I'd had my heart kicked."

"You've got it all wrong, Zeke," Linda insisted. "*I* was the one who was brokenhearted. You told me to go away, remember?"

Zeke smirked and crossed his arms. "Who-suffered-more contests usually don't solve things."

"I couldn't agree more," Linda said. She bit back the lump forming in her throat as she realized how much he'd misunderstood what had happened. "I guess you must have hated me."

"Hated you?" Zeke asked, the amazed look on his face speaking volumes. "I couldn't, Lindy. But I'm not willing to go through it all over again. Don't worry. I'll leave you alone just as soon as I finish with your banister."

Linda felt an overwhelming flood of disappointment. Just when things were beginning to come clear to her, he was cutting off contact. But maybe that was wise, she conceded. She had feared becoming too attached to Zeke again herself.

"Fine," she bit out. She tried to think of something more to say, something final and meaningful, but no words came. Just tears that she didn't want Zeke to see. She pivoted and headed for the living room.

"I gotta go upstairs," Seth said as she passed him in the hallway.

"Me, too," his brother echoed.

Linda looked at them suspiciously. "Are you guys okay?"

"Uh-huh," Seth said.

"I wanna take a nap." Both little boys trudged quietly up the stairs.

"I'll check on you as soon as I've seen to Emily," Linda said. "Hey, maybe I'll read you a story." They only grunted in return to that idea, which worried and annoyed her. They liked it when Zeke read to them!

She went over to the playpen to check Emily's diaper. Of course it was wet. She picked up the baby and started upstairs.

The diaper knack came easily enough now so that Linda could wool-gather while tending to Emily. She thought hard about Zeke and tried stoically to convince herself that things were for the best. She wasn't going to let a man—*especially* not Zeke Howell—break her heart again.

"You've got to be careful of that little heart of yours," she instructed Emily as she fastened the last pin.

Dry and happy, Emily smiled back absently. The tiny fingers of one hand reached out to Linda's pinky and made a fist around it. As her niece clutched tightly to her, Linda felt her mouth go dry with awe. There was a lot of power in that little finger.

She picked up the baby and patted her soft little back as she walked her over to the cradle. Not for the first time during her visit, she wondered about all the things life promised that she'd ignored. Love, marriage, babies. Emily could probably teach her more about heartbreak than she knew.

"Aunt Lindy! Aunt Lindy!"

Linda hurriedly laid Emily in her crib and raced down the hall toward the twins. When she entered their room, they were both sitting up in their beds, their skin matching the scaly green dinosaurs on their comforters.

"I'm sick."

"Me, too."

Linda told herself to be calm as she reached over to touch one forehead, then the other. They both felt hot. But then, so did her own forehead, perhaps because she was so nervous.

"I need to get a thermometer. I'll be right back."

"I think I'm dying," Seth said.

Dying? "No, you're not," she answered hurriedly, feeling her panic rising. "I'm going to call a doctor." She remembered the notepad by the kitchen phone, the one Naomi had written all the emergency numbers on, and bolted for the door.

"Aunt Lindy..."

At the tortured sound, she ran back. Saul looked up at her with distressed blue eyes welling with tears. "Can we keep Hippo?" he asked, his little voice muzzy and weak.

Linda dropped to her knees and hugged the little boy's shoulders. Words couldn't describe the agony she felt just seeing the pain on the little boy's face. "Of course."

"You'll talk to Mama?" Seth asked.

"Yes, I promise. Now, sweetie, I have to call the doctor."

She got up and rushed down the stairs. Zeke stared at her in alarm.

"What's wrong?"

Suddenly, it was all too much for her. Linda launched herself against Zeke's strong chest and held tight. Choking back sobs, she angled him toward the kitchen and the phone pad.

"I've got to call the doctor. The twins are very sick!"

"Are you sure?" Zeke asked. "They looked fine just a minute ago."

"They're green!" Linda cried as she scanned the list. She grabbed the phone and nervously began to punch buttons.

"Lindy." Zeke took the receiver from her and hung it up. "How many brownies did they eat?"

"Brownies!" Linda cried, not quite making the connection. When she finally did, it seemed that a weight was lifted off her shoulders. "Oh."

"'Oh' is right. Those guys probably scarfed down a stomachful, and now they're paying for it. I should have warned you."

"I should have thought..."

He kept hold of her arm as they walked back up the stairs together, and for that, Linda was glad. It felt so good to lean on someone.

"What did you guys do?" Zeke boomed as he walked between the twin beds. "You decided to become like the Cookie Monster?"

"Zeke, guess what?" Seth sat up excitedly, apparently having made a miraculous recovery. "Aunt Lindy said we could keep Hippo!"

"She promised!"

Slowly Zeke turned to her. "She did?"

On either side of him, the twins beamed at her with sly little grins. No doubt about it, she'd been had.

"I guess I did," she admitted.

Linda sank onto the end of Saul's bed, worried about how she would explain this to Naomi. And worried, too, about how swiftly she'd found so much comfort in Zeke's arms.

Chapter Five

No matter how hard Linda tried, the words "I'm giving the twins a kitten for their birthday" wouldn't come out of her mouth. She just couldn't do it, even though this was her second chance in as many days.

Outside the window, the two boys were playing with the kitten in the late-morning sun. Meanwhile, over the phone, Naomi worried on about poor Mrs. Ward and William, who were understandably inconsolable.

"Mrs. Ward wasn't even eating until today."

"That's terrible," Linda said. She remembered the pain she'd felt after her mother's death. But that probably didn't compare to losing a spouse.

With all Naomi's troubles, there was no way that Linda could tell her about the kitten...or any of the things that had led up to her agreeing to let the twins keep Hippo. Knowing Naomi, she wouldn't let her stop explaining until she had heard about the washing machine, the basement, the banister, the brownies and goodness knew what else. And instinctively, Naomi would know about her and Zeke.

But what exactly was there to know? The banister had been finished a day and a half ago; Zeke was gone. As promised, Linda hadn't heard from him for an entire day, and for all she knew, she never would again.

Naomi had never liked Zeke, Linda knew. Ever the one-sided, loyal sister, she'd always blamed him for breaking her heart. She would have little sympathy toward his recent disappearance, except to say it was wise that they didn't see each other again. So Linda kept the sadness she felt to herself.

"How are the kids?" came the voice from the receiver.

Linda tensed. It was now or never. Never, she decided. "They're fine."

"You're certainly not very talkative today. You weren't Wednesday night when I called, either. Is something wrong?"

"Of course not!" Linda hastened to assure her. She didn't have any more courage now than she'd had the night before last, when Naomi had first called to check on the kids. Right after Zeke had left. "Everything's fine. I've got it all under control here. What do you have planned for today?"

After giving Linda the day's itinerary and assurances that she and William would be home that night, Naomi said goodbye.

For a moment, after putting down the receiver, Linda ruminated on marriage. What must it be like to be so in sync with another person, like Naomi and William? She sometimes wondered whether she was missing out on something. But marriage seemed such a complicated enterprise.

She was lucky to have escaped it, Linda consoled herself. Not that marriage had been too difficult to dodge; the truth was, she just hadn't had that many offers. How could she, with all her energies focused on work? Which was exactly where they should be focused now, she decided. If there was one thing she'd discovered in the past days, it was the danger of getting sidetracked. She'd spent far too much time thinking about Zeke, and silly what-ifs like marriage and children, and too little time with her nose to the grindstone.

She should call Jane. And then, this afternoon, she would sit down with her personal planner and come up with twenty business goals to work toward in the next year. She could easily fit that activity in between lunch and "Mr. Roger's Neighborhood."

That way, she would leave herself no time to mope about missing Zeke, which didn't even make sense. She hadn't seen him at all for nearly thirteen years and had survived just fine. Now, after just over a day, she was completely down in the dumps.

Linda dragged her coffee cup over to the kitchen table and flipped to the business section of the paper. She stared at it unseeing for a moment, wool-gathering again. She had to stop that!

The back door opened, and, without looking up from an article on corporate America's meanest bosses, Linda instructed, "Don't forget to wipe your feet."

"Yes, ma'am."

The deep voice wasn't at all what she expected. Linda pivoted in her chair and then jumped up. "Zeke, what are you doing here?"

He leaned back against a counter, resting his elbows on the Formica behind him, and sent her an almost belligerent stare. "I'm going to fix your bathroom sink."

"It leaks," Linda said.

"That's why I'm going to fix it."

"I see." Was that the only reason he'd come back? She walked cautiously over to a neighboring counter to see whether she could find out. Over her coffee cup, she mused, "You know, I'm only a visitor here. It could be that Naomi likes leaks."

"Tough." His green eyes sparked with challenge.

Linda cocked her head to the side and smiled. Her heart was racing a million miles a minute. "Weren't you the one who said it would be better if we didn't see each other?"

Zeke's face reddened, and he looked down at his feet for a moment, as if the answer to that question could be found in the worn leather toe of his work boots.

"You must really like to fix things," Linda teased.

Zeke cleared his throat. "You know, there's an old saying about looking a gift horse in the mouth."

"I remember that one," Linda answered. "But then there's also the old story about the Trojan horse, where the gift horse turned out to be a way for them to storm their enemy's barriers."

Zeke edged closer. "Am I the enemy?"

His eyes were piercing and dark, and this time Linda was the one who looked away.

"And is that what you think I'm doing, storming your barriers?"

When she looked back up at him, he had an amused grin on his face. "Maybe," she said.

"Then you'd better keep a close watch on me," he advised.

"Do you think I haven't been doing that already?" Before he could answer, she asked, "Will you have a cup of coffee?"

"No, thanks," he said, taking her abrupt change of topic in stride. "I've had mine."

"In that case, we'd both better get to work," Linda said.

She began to walk away, but he caught her by the arm and cut off her exit. "Not so fast," he said. "I want to talk to you."

"About what?" Linda asked warily.

"Everything."

She skeptically lifted an eyebrow. "Well, I don't know how much I can tell you about that, since we're not supposed to see each other anymore."

A hint of a smile played around the edges of his mouth. "Is that what you're so wound up about?"

"I'm not wound up!" she said, her manner contradicting her meaning. She sprang back from him. "Can I help being a little off balance at the way you breeze in and out as if—"

"As if what?" Frowning, he reached out to her again, as if he could capture the end of her thought in his hand.

"Never mind."

"No, go on." Linda backed up until she collided with a cabinet, and Zeke followed her, step for step. "You think I'm breezing in and out of here like I own the place, is that it?"

"No."

"Then what?"

"As if you take it for granted that I'm always going to be here," Linda bit out.

Zeke backed off and stretched against the counter again, looking supremely pleased with her answer. "I would never take you for granted, Lindy. We've both been away too long."

"Then—"

"Look," he explained, putting a hand squarely on each of her shoulders. "I didn't come back here to make a move on you or anything like that. There's been a lot of water under the bridge in thirteen years. But I felt like a damned fool staying away from you, Lindy, knowing you were just blocks away. I missed you."

Lindy stared up at him in wonder—both for his brave confession and for the way he had known exactly how she was feeling before she had a chance to tell him. She thought again about how some people—very married people—got that much in sync. Zeke's whole effect on her life made her nervous. Yet she didn't want to do without him, either. Not just yet.

"There's no reason why we can't be friends," she agreed. "Since we're both here together."

"That's right," Zeke said. Holding her, no matter how chastely, was the agony he'd longed for during the past thirty-six hours. "Friends," he gritted out.

Linda was careful not to look too closely into those green eyes of his, fearful they would reveal exactly what she felt inside. That being friends just wasn't enough. Not after what they'd been to each other. But it was better than not getting to see him at all.

At least, it was the adult thing to do. Which reminded her, it was high time she started behaving like one again. She ducked her shoulders from beneath his grasp. Just because they were going to be in contact with each other—strictly as friends—was no reason to completely abandon her game plan for the afternoon.

"I've got to call the office," she said, turning away from him. "And I assume this is just your lunch hour."

"Correct," he said.

"Then maybe we should talk—about everything, if that's what you want—later."

He once again stopped her with a hand on her arm. "Only if later means this evening."

"Yes, all right," Linda said, avoiding eye contact. Her stare was fixed on his hand, as though by looking she could remove it from her person. "I'll make dinner or something."

Zeke let out a heartfelt sigh as he let her go and watched her scurry away, but he wasn't at all unhappy with the way his morning had gone. He'd learned some important things today. One, that while they were in the same town, he couldn't possibly stay away from Lindy longer than twenty-four hours. And two, that the lady wasn't yet sick of the sight of him. That was something, he supposed.

He mussed the twins' red heads on his way out to the truck to retrieve his toolbox, whistling all the way. And when Mrs. Huckabee peeked out her eyelet window curtain, he shot her a broad wink that even her twelve-year-old bifocals couldn't obscure. She stared, stunned, and then tossed her head back to laugh.

"Zeke? Are you going to be working here again?" Seth asked. The day before yesterday, Zeke had told them that he was finished with his work there.

"I sure am," he hollered back as he took the porch steps two at a time. He was working on a lot of things, not the least of which was trying to figure out whether Lindy shared some of the same feelings he did.

He heard her talking on the phone as he passed by the living room and unconsciously slowed his steps. There was something different about this conversation than the ones he'd heard her having with her employees before. This time it sounded as if she actually had something to say.

In the next room, Linda refocused her attention, which had temporarily been diverted by the sight of Zeke breezily crossing through the hallway. She didn't know which made her happier—Jane's news, or the fact that Zeke had obviously felt the need to trump up a reason to visit her.

"Tell me again," she asked Jane, "did you say they wanted a three-month trial basis?"

"The hunk's there, isn't he?"

"Never mind that," Linda said in a low voice. "It's been a while since we've snagged a company as large as Advantage Microchips."

"You're right," Jane agreed. "And according to this Mr. Ryan I spoke to, the employees they shuttle back and forth to Silicon Valley could almost constitute a whole new airline."

Linda brimmed with satisfaction at those words. "That mailing was a great idea."

"If you do say so yourself."

"And I do." Linda sank onto the familiar sofa and frowned. "I wish I were there."

But the words were forced. What truly worried her was the fact that she didn't mind not being back at the office. Even as Jane had bubbled over with the news of their big new corporate account, Linda had been listening for Zeke's footsteps, tapping her pen absently to the sound of his whistle, wondering what he and the twins were saying. This wasn't like her.

Distractions were something that she ceased to allow herself years ago. So maybe her life had become more humdrum because of her single-mindedness, and it certainly hadn't made for a swinging social life, but wasn't her business worth it?

"Linda?"

She zeroed back in on the voice of her friend. "I'm sorry, what was I saying?"

"That you wished you were here," Jane said in an ironic tone. "Then you blipped off."

That was just the problem, Linda thought. As long as she allowed herself to indulge in her infatuation with Zeke, she would forever be blipping off. "I should set up my fax," she said purposefully. It was sitting in the trunk of her car, awaiting a big emergency.

"Why?" Jane asked. "You're supposed to be on vacation."

"Yes, but important things are happening."

"We're handling it fine," Jane argued.

Although she couldn't say why, the words rankled Linda. Maybe it still hurt her to think that her baby, her business, was getting along fine without her. Maybe it was because Zeke chose that moment to saunter through the hallway again on the way to his truck. And maybe, probably, it was because she was feeling a little torn between the two.

"I'll never have time to drink all that lemonade, George."

George Warren rested his back against the eaves of the Bledsoes' roof and poured himself a big cup from the thermos of lemonade he'd brought up for Zeke. Having risked life and limb to get up on this fool roof, he wasn't about to crawl down again anytime soon. "Why?" he asked. "You got somewhere to go?"

"Yup." Zeke pounded in a nail.

George scratched his head. "That somewhere wouldn't be anywheres in the vicinity of Sycamore Street, would it?"

"Yup."

The older man chuckled. "Not a bad street. I go there sometimes myself."

"To gossip with Vera, you mean?" Zeke didn't want to have this conversation. He was already too wound up about seeing Lindy. To have George tell him he was being a fool was not something he relished.

"You bet. Vera's had some mighty interesting things to say recently about the goings-on next door. Like this mornin' she said that you'd winked at her from next door like you was the happiest man alive. And only yesterday you was telling me that you'd had it with the Potter woman." George's eyes narrowed like a hawk's coming down on prey. "So. What do you have to be so happy about?"

"Not a thing, George," Zeke said. "Not a thing."

"Vera said—"

Zeke rolled his eyes and put down his hammer. "Okay, okay. I'm having dinner at Lindy's tonight. There. Now you have some news for your girlfriend."

"Where'd you hear Vera was my girlfriend?" George asked suspiciously. "I've been a bachelor for sixty-plus years."

"A bachelor who's been wearing out his Out to Lunch sign lately."

George stared at him long and hard, then waved a hand dismissively. "Aw, you don't know anything." He pulled his pipe from his hip pocket and lit it. "You said you and Lindy were all washed up on account of her being such a hotshot and all."

"She just owns a business," Zeke defended. "That hardly makes her Ivana Trump."

"And what about that little sports car she zips around town in? Dwight Doggett was over the other day, saying that he's already given her a ticket."

"A parking ticket, George."

"Humph. Still shows that you and her have different ways of looking at things."

"How?" Zeke asked testily. The older man had succeeded in getting his goat. "It's just a parking ticket! Good Lord, if you're so determined to ring some kind of significance out of every little thing, try this—I just plain like her. I always have. Besides, we're just friends."

George took a long tug of tobacco. "Just friends, huh?"

"Yeah."

The storekeeper shook his head sadly. "That won't last long."

"Why not?" Zeke asked. He'd been having the same hunch himself.

"'Cause sooner or later—and probably sooner—one or the other of you will decide you want to be more than 'friends.' And then you'll either be making hay while the sun shines or you won't be speaking to each other. Leastways, you won't be friends."

The man's logic was faultless. Zeke let out a sigh and raked an arm across his sweaty forehead. "I hope you're wrong, George. But if you aren't, I'll opt for making hay over stone silence."

"Figured that." George took another suck on his pipe. "So I don't see why you just don't say so, instead of messing around with all this 'friends' business. I just want to see how it all comes out."

"And whether you're going to have more afternoons off for fishing or not." Although, judging from the pungent after-shave wafting across the rooftop, Zeke wondered whether fishing was all the old guy had on his mind after all. Maybe he'd figured George wrong.

"You said that before," George accused, "and it just isn't true. I don't want to see you torn up again, is all." He met Zeke's gaze over his pipe, then looked away. "You seemed like you were getting yourself together. You still going to take that class on restoring old houses over at Tyler?"

"Yes, I am."

"If you was to go in on the store with me, you'd have more money to do what you wanted. And don't think I wouldn't give you equal time off."

"I know that, George."

They sat in silence for a moment. Finally George sighed and said, "I guess maybe I just don't want you to leave. It's been good to have you back, son."

Knowing both of them would be uncomfortable if he just gushed out his feelings, Zeke looked away quickly, over the roofs of Grover's Springs. If he squinted into the distance, he could see the landmarks around his own house. Home. This was where he belonged.

"I'm not leaving, George," he said finally, clearing his throat. "For better or worse, I'm here now."

"Does Lindy Potter know that?"

"Maybe not," Zeke replied. "But she will."

As he hopped up the front steps of the old wood-frame house that evening, Zeke tried telling himself that he wasn't being a fool. But the dazzling purple irises in his hand said something entirely different. They screamed "boyfriend" when he was still trying to keep it casual.

He was dressed casual, at least. His new but respectably faded jeans hugged his legs nonchalantly, and even though he wore a short-sleeved button-down instead of a T-shirt, he didn't think it looked particularly formal. And his boots were good and worn in.

No, what was really making him stiff was the way he felt inside. Nervous, as if he was going on a date or something instead of just visiting Lindy and the kids for the evening. And then there were those flowers, which he probably shouldn't have brought. He'd just felt like picking them because they reminded him somehow of her. Because they were wild looking, striking . . . pretty.

He self-consciously held the flowers behind his back and rapped on the door with his other hand. For a long minute, no one answered, which made him even more anxious. When the door finally did swing open, no one was visible at eye level. Zeke looked down into Saul's face.

Instead of saying hello, the child screamed "Zeke's here!" at the top of his little lungs. He blocked the doorway. "What's that in your hand?" he asked.

"Oh, flowers." Zeke shuffled the irises forward for Saul's inspection.

The child twisted his mouth into a frown. His brother came skidding up from the living room, took a look at Zeke, then turned back toward the staircase. "Aunt Lindy, Zeke's here!" he yelled.

Zeke cleared his throat. "May I come in?"

In unison, the two boys shook their heads.

"Are those flowers?" Seth asked distastefully.

Something weird was happening. Had Lindy given the boys instructions not to allow him in? Maybe she was angry at the way he'd let himself into the kitchen this afternoon. Or maybe she really didn't want to see him.

He inched the flowers behind his back again and for a moment even considered stowing them behind the azalea shrub a few feet away. Then Lindy descended the stairs, holding Emily. Only she didn't look like Lindy... not the one he was used to now, at any rate.

In a blue suit complete with stockings and medium-heeled navy pumps, she looked like something out of corporate America. Her short jacket hugged her torso, as did the knee-length skirt, and those heels did dazzling things for her legs. Her hair even complemented the outfit—while in her casual clothes it looked funky, now the short, neat locks made her look sharp and well-groomed. He felt a little shabby, and suddenly wondered about his choice to be casual.

But then, why was Lindy dressing for success in Grover's Springs?

"Boys, why didn't you show Zeke in?" she asked the twins.

"Mommy said we shouldn't let people come into the house," Seth answered.

"Oh." Lindy looked up at Zeke and shrugged apologetically. "Sorry." She shuffled the children to the side with her free hand and gestured Zeke in. He shut the door behind himself and followed her to the living room. "Actually," she said, "I lost track of time. I got involved in work, then laundry and then the baby..."

What shred of self-confidence Zeke had left was deflating rapidly.

"What's that in your hand?" Linda asked as she put Emily down in her playpen. "Are those irises?"

"Yeah," Zeke answered, shuffling forward, "I brought them for you."

"You bought them?" she asked, misunderstanding.

"No, I picked them."

Linda's eyes widened. "I hope you didn't steal them." Thoughts of Mrs. Huckabee's blooming flower beds crossed her mind.

"Of course I didn't," Zeke retorted tightly. What did she think he was, a hoodlum?

"I only meant from someone's yard," Linda explained. "Knowing how Mrs. Huckabee loves her flowers, she'd have a fit. But at least they aren't pansies."

"I didn't steal them," Zeke repeated.

"Well, anyway," Linda said, "I'll go put them in water now."

What was he so huffy about? Linda wondered as she walked to the kitchen, at the same time realizing that she was on edge herself. Getting back into her work clothes had reminded her that she really didn't belong here, no matter how whimsical she felt, playing mom for a week to the twins and baby Emily. And she had no business leading Zeke along, even under their new "friends" ruse.

As she stuffed the irises into their new home, she caught Zeke's reflection in the glass of the vase. He was hanging back in the kitchen doorway. No man on earth looked as good in a pair of dungarees as Zeke did, Linda observed as she pretended to arrange the flowers. No man made her feel more vulnerable, either.

"I want to take you somewhere," Zeke said.

Linda turned, trying to pretend she hadn't known he was standing there. Her insides felt all churned up. It was as if her life, which had been floating in a steady stream of water, were suddenly being sucked into a gigantic, turbulent whirlpool, with Zeke at its center.

"I can't—"

"The kids can come, too," Zeke assured her, anticipating her response as he had that afternoon.

"Yeah, but look—"

"So change." He meant her clothes, which is exactly what she had been about to use as an excuse. And of course, before she could voice her next objection, he had to add, "Borrow something from Naomi."

"I don't know..."

"What don't you know about, Lindy?" Zeke answered. "Me? How you feel about me?"

"This is weird, Zeke," she answered frankly. "I mean, I'd just gotten to the point where I never thought about you anymore. I mean, hardly ever. I've got a life back in Dallas, and I like it the way it is. Our both being back in Grover's Springs together is just a fluke. You'll probably be blowing out of town one of these days yourself."

"Lindy, there's something I really want to show you."

"It's not going to change things, Zeke," she said harshly. It felt good to speak her mind finally, after tiptoeing around the old baggage between them for days now. "Neither of us belongs here. We don't belong together."

He smiled. "Are you sure about that?"

"I almost think I'm sure."

Zeke crossed his arms, glad to hear that she was definitely not definite on this point. "I think there's something that might change the equation."

She rolled her eyes. "Zeke..."

"Trust me," he said, sensing her weakening. "There's something I have to show you."

"Okay, I give in," Lindy said. She was game—besides, it would be great to get out. "What is it?"

Zeke hesitated, then smiled. "My house."

Chapter Six

Linda gasped with recognition as Zeke swerved his pickup onto a short dirt road. The brushy lane was even shabbier than she remembered, though someone had clearly chopped back some of the growth.

"This is the way to your old place!" she exclaimed.

One of Zeke's eyebrows shot up amusedly. "Where did you think 'my house' was, exactly?"

"I don't know...."

Not here, that was for darn sure. Never here. She shut her eyes against seeing the old ramshackle clapboard house Zeke had both loved and hated while growing up. The place was sure to have deteriorated in the years Zeke had been gone. She couldn't imagine what he was doing living out here. Torturing himself?

Before she could ask, the truck rounded a sharp corner that opened onto a little rundown neighborhood that consisted of five houses spread out over fifteen or so acres, all connected with dusty dirt paths. Only, when

Linda opened her eyes, she wasn't looking at the ramshackle mess that used to be the Howell house. Something, something verging on the magical, had transformed the house.

"Home again, home again," Zeke joked, killing the engine. He looked at her sideways to gauge her reaction.

"Jiggedy-jig," Linda mumbled blankly as she hugged Emily and took in the sight before her. A coat of white paint had done wonders for the little house, which she was slowly beginning to recognize as the Howell place she remembered. New shutters were painted a deep burgundy color, and the roof she could tell had been recently redone. She used to think that the house looked miserable, gray and saggy, but in its new incarnation, the modest story-and-a-half structure stood proudly erect, as though someone had given it a whopper of a pep talk.

"I can't believe it," she whispered.

"Is this where you live, Zeke?" Seth asked, poking his head up to see over the dashboard.

"It's not as big as our house," Saul observed.

Zeke laughed. "I guess bigger is better?"

"Always," Seth answered for his twin.

"Well, come have a look-see, anyway," Zeke said as he stepped down from the pickup and helped the twins out. Linda busied herself with getting Emily settled into the stroller they had stowed in the bed of the truck.

"I'm amazed by what you've done here, Zeke," she said as she reached the porch, where Zeke had installed a rejuvenated porch swing. "It's like a miracle."

"The miracle was that my father managed not to lose the family's only asset," Zeke replied sharply. "When I found that out after he died, I figured it was a sign."

"A sign?" Linda asked as she stepped over the threshold.

"To come home."

She shuddered to think what Zeke must have found when he came back to Grover's Springs those months ago, but the place looked like a home now. Though it was sparsely furnished, Zeke had refurbished the inside as thoroughly as the exterior. Bright white walls and woodwork gleamed in the entrance hallway, and the hardwood floors had been stripped, stained a light brown and polished to a high gloss.

The twins ran immediately toward the small stairwell tucked into the corner of the hall, which led to the two small upstairs rooms. There was an archway beyond the stairs that Linda didn't remember being there. Instead of checking it out, however, she pushed the stroller disbelievingly into the living room, where her expectations, more than her eyes, took a moment to adjust to walls that had been painted a pale cheery yellow. She could barely imagine the Zeke she knew—Zeke of the faded jeans and husky voice—moving about in such a place, much less designing it!

But as he strolled in behind her, looking supremely pleased and at ease in the surprisingly spacious room, Linda's skepticism fell away. Especially when he smiled one of those winning smiles at her and turned to the window.

"Great view," he said, and he was right. The tangle of honeysuckle, dogwood and just plain weeds along the lane formed a giant green hedge, and the property was dotted with healthy old elms and oaks, which dappled the house and sprawling yard with shade.

"Originally I thought I'd just fix the place up so I could sell it," he continued. "But the more time I spent replacing boards and roofing and painting, the more I doubted I'd be able to turn it over to strangers."

"You always dreamed of fixing it up," Linda said, coming to stand beside him at the window.

"That's the strange thing. I wasn't doing it consciously. But when I came out of the paint store one day, I realized I'd picked out my mother's favorite shade of yellow for the living room. And after I had finished the floors, I remembered I'd always hated the way they used to look like brown mud. Without meaning to, I made the place into the kind of bright airy house I'd always dreamed it could be when I was a kid."

"I think it's terrific. It makes me want to live here."

Zeke rubbed his jaw thoughtfully and pierced her with his green eyes. "Does it?"

Linda paled. "Well...you know what I mean. I'm so used to cramped rented town houses where everything's yuppie beige."

Zeke shrugged and turned his gaze back outside. "The only thing I did consciously was the back porch. Daddy always wanted to put one of those in."

"You built a porch? By yourself?"

Zeke laughed. "It's what I do, you know. I build things."

"I thought you just...fixed."

"Because that's where the money mostly has been around here, but restoring is where my real interest is. I've taken quite a few college architecture courses along the way, ones that focus on the restoration of old homes."

"Oh." Linda was impressed, but not at all surprised. Zeke had never been one to stop wanting to do more. "You have to show me the porch."

He ushered her back to the hall. On the other side of the house was the kitchen and another small room, but they went back to the archway beyond the staircase.

"This used to be the back wall!" Linda remembered.

"Yeah, I had to knock out the space for a door."

As they crossed the doorway, Linda couldn't believe her eyes. The porch looking onto the backyard was lined with huge picture windows. The wall to her right was dominated by a bay window and window seat, which she immediately ran over to inspect.

"This is so neat!"

"I think it turned out well," Zeke said, crossing his arms and surveying his handiwork with a satisfied eye.

Suddenly, Linda gasped aloud as she took in the world beyond all the glass. Honeysuckle lined a rather dilapidated fence, one side of which sagged under the burden of a bank of Cherokee roses. But the most spectacular thing about the yard was the volume of flowers jutting up from the ground—daisies and snapdragons, marigolds, larkspurs, irises . . . she couldn't even put names to all the bright plants that caught her gaze. Linda was overwhelmed by the richness of their colors blending together.

Zeke laughed. "After I first saw what an awful mess this place was in, I went straight to the nursery and spent probably a week's pay on seeds alone. I figured if I was going to have to work on the place, it would be nice to have a little color to look at."

"You certainly have color now!" Linda exclaimed. "I want to go outside."

Just then, the clomping sounds of the twins coming back down the stairs rang through the house. "Aunt Lindy, go upstairs!" one of them cried in advance of his appearance. Seth bounded into the room. "His bathtub has feet!"

"Scary feet," Saul said, right behind him.

"C'mon," Zeke said. He bent down and effortlessly scooped Saul up to his hip, whipped open the door and took Seth by the hand. "I'll show you two my old swing."

Mentioning that last word apparently wiped all thought of evil bathtubs out of the kids' heads, because they were instantly eager to see Zeke's playground. Linda was, too, and as she followed them out into the yard, struggling with the bulky stroller down the porch steps, she wondered again at how deft Zeke was with children. He seemed to know exactly what to say, and just what they would be most interested in. As though he'd given a lot of thought to having children one day. Or maybe he was still part child himself....

For a fleeting, astonishing moment, she wished that she had heard the tick-tick-ticking of her biological clock, so she would know whether she was ready to settle down and have a family. It seemed such a gigantic step, when she'd been busy all her life pursuing different goals. Yet she knew she wanted to have a meaningful relationship in her life. What would happen if the man of her dreams wanted to have more than a wife and her business? What if he also wanted babies in the bargain? What if she had to decide now?

More slowly she approached the tire swing, hanging from a giant oak's limb. "This was your swing?" she asked anxiously. It was only a tire tied to the tree by a length of hefty rope, yet the twins were going to town on it, with Seth inside the ring of the circle and Saul riding on top.

"Don't worry, it's a new tire and new rope," Zeke assured her. "It's the same old spot where mine was, though. I couldn't imagine this backyard without it here."

Linda nodded, understanding the wistful feeling completely. As the twins spun sloppily around, squealing with glee, she remembered herself and Naomi playing like that on a swing in the municipal park as children. They'd begged their father for a swing in their yard, but he'd never taken to the idea. He preferred to keep the property pristine. Maybe she could convince Naomi to put one in.

Right, she thought wryly. She'd approach Naomi about that one just after she told her about Hippo the tiger cat....

"I want to go hunt bugs!" Seth yelled. Abruptly he and his brother bailed out of the swing and tore off across the yard.

Zeke steadied the swing with one hand and gestured with the other in a flourish. "Care to take a spin?"

"Oh, I don't know...." But she did. Before she could think better of it, she stepped onto the tire and pushed off.

"Hey!" Zeke cried in surprise, chuckling as he stepped out of her path. "Have a seat and I'll give you a push."

"You'll have to catch me first!" Linda yelled back. She pushed off again, then hit the tree with her foot, sending the tire spinning in an unwieldy circle. She laughed at the dizzying sensation, then caught sight of Zeke approaching from behind the tree trunk. Pushing again with her foot, she set her course directly at him in a kamikaze attack. Zeke dove out of her way.

"Chicken!" she yelled.

"Oh, yeah?" Before she could turn toward his voice, a large hand clamped down on the rope before her face, jolting the swing to a halt. Suddenly, he was in front of her.

"This is how I remember you, Lindy," Zeke said. His face was neither smiling nor unhappy; there was just intense concentration in his eyes.

Linda shifted uncomfortably on the swing, realizing suddenly that she might have put a little too much stress on her healing ankle. She looped a leg over the top so that she was in a sitting position. "How?" she asked. "I'll bet you money that we never once played on a tire swing in high school."

"You know what I mean," Zeke replied. "It's not what you're doing, it's how you're acting."

"Like a juvenile," Linda quipped. "Thanks."

He set her in motion again with a gentle shove of the swing. "That's not what I meant."

"I know," Linda said more seriously. He meant that she was Crazy Lindy no more. But he, unlike she, had forgotten the reasons she'd said good riddance to that persona. And if she had, her aching ankle from their tire swing antics just now would have reminded her. "I'm not a high school kid, Zeke. I can't run around behaving like one—I have responsibilities."

"All work and no play?" Zeke asked. He reined in the swing and rested one of his feet in the circle of the tire.

Linda was almost getting used to the disturbing feeling she had every time Zeke was this near. "It used to be the other way around, and look what happened to us. That accident of ours was like a diploma welcoming me to the real world, Zeke. Isn't it better now that we're behaving reasonably?"

Zeke let out a sad little sigh. "I guess *reasonably* means you don't want me to kiss you."

"Zeke!"

"Okay, okay," he mumbled good-naturedly. He stepped away and started pushing her again so that she ran a loop around him in slow gentle circles. Still, he looked sad that she had cut off their moment of flirtation; the way Linda felt inside.

"I know what your problem is," she said. "You've got twin envy."

Zeke raised his sagging head. "What's that?"

"It's the same thing I've had all week. The insatiable desire to be five years old again."

In the corner of the yard the twins were deeply involved in their bug-catching endeavor. Zeke couldn't see that they were having much luck, even though the yard was crawling with more kinds of insect life than he cared to think about. But although twenty-five years back he'd been a pretty intrepid ladybug hunter, he was afraid his "insatiable desires" now had little to do with that long-lost skill, or anything remotely interesting to a five-year-old. They had everything to do with the woman on the swing.

Nevertheless, he nodded in understanding. "I guess they are carefree."

"About everything!" Linda said enthusiastically. "All they have to do is dress themselves in the morning and they've done their day's work. And sometimes I have to help them with that! The rest of their time is spent tearing around the house, tearing up the yard, to the point where I'm ready to tear out my hair. During their peaceful moments they sing along with a dancing purple dinosaur on television."

"Come to think of it, it must be nice to be light-years from reality."

"And you should see what those little bodies can scarf down!" She grimaced. "Unfortunately, I'm afraid I've been scarfing right along with them. I've probably gained five pounds in Captain Crunch alone."

"Kids are fun," Zeke said. "Whenever I'm working on a house, they follow me around like I'm the Pied Piper or something, asking endless questions."

"That's why you're so good with them, then."

"I'm just more used to talking to them than you are. Me, I've never used a fax machine, but I imagine it's not that hard to figure out."

"Yeah, but kids actually *like* you," Linda countered. "I've been around the twins all week and we're still not always in sync." She looked over to the quiet stroller in dismay. "And I'm afraid Emily and I have a shaky rapport at best. I can't always count on her to laugh at my jokes, and she's always either sleeping or crying."

Zeke let out a hearty laugh and gave her another shove. "She's just a baby, Lindy. Sleeping and crying are what babies do best."

"That's what Jane says," Linda shot back doubtfully. She rested her temple against the thick rough rope and looked at Zeke again. All his talk about kids made him sound as though he wished he were a family man. Linda never would have guessed it from knowing him thirteen years ago. True, people changed. She just wanted to know how much.

"Why haven't you gotten married, Zeke?" The words rang awkwardly through the air, yet Linda was immediately glad she'd asked. Maybe she'd been wanting to ask all week.

"Why haven't you?" He looked tense and regarded her through narrowed eyes.

Linda stubbed her toe against the rich green grass and stopped the swing. Now that they were finally getting to the heart of matters, she didn't want to be twisting and looping. "I asked first," she countered.

Zeke folded his arms across his chest and cleared his throat. Before he spoke, his jaw worked for a moment so that a dimple appeared by his mouth. It had been there all along, but Linda had never noticed it before.

"I guess..." He cleared his throat again, then, looking down, shuffled a foot across the tips of the grass. "I guess I was just too busy moving around. Seeing the world, like we said."

Linda nodded, but she knew he was telling only a half-truth.

"What about you?" he asked. "Seems like women decide what they want faster than men."

Linda had to laugh at that bit of sociological speculation. She could only wish it were true. "Have you been watching those talk shows, too?" she joked.

Zeke frowned, then stared back at her with widening eyes, as if he were amazed. "You mean, you haven't decided whether you want to get married and have kids yet?"

"It's not like I'm a dinosaur, Zeke," Linda retorted in an ironic tone. "I do have a few years left in me before I become fossilized. I suppose there are large chunks of my life I still haven't made up my mind about yet."

Zeke felt his face redden; she'd misunderstood him completely. He was overjoyed by the news that her life was still in flux. That meant that he still had time to influence her future plans, which apparently weren't as set in stone as she let on most of the time. Maybe he was even part of that chunk she was talking about.

All week long he'd been working on the assumption that it was probably too late for him and Linda to pursue anything other than nostalgia. Sure he'd hoped, but every time he began to get a little too hopeful, she would hop on the phone or drag out her fax machine and remind him that he was just an old flame whom she'd parted ways with long ago. Now she was hinting that there was a possibility for more, and he wasn't one to let possibilities pass him by.

"I've always thought I would have children—someday," Linda said, filling in the silence. She grimaced. "But I guess that's not very specific."

"I hope you've been specific enough to plan for a husband sometime before having those kids," Zeke said.

Linda shot him one of her old you've-got-to-be-kidding glances. "If there's one thing I've learned, it's that a person needs all the support staff she can get."

Zeke laughed at her comparison. "So I suppose you still plan to be boss after you've hooked a family?"

"You bet." Briefly, Linda remembered the blissful day after she'd sprained her ankle. It had been a nice change to let someone else buzz around taking care of things for once. "Although I might settle for an alternative role, like queen bee."

He stepped closer, forcing her to look him square in the eye. "Tell me the truth, Lindy," he said. "Why haven't you married?"

"I've told you. My work—"

"I refuse to believe making money can mean that much to you. That's not like you."

When he put it that way, Linda could hardly refute him without sounding like a soulless miser. Not only that, he was staring at her again with those intense green eyes. There was no way she could lie to those eyes. "All right," she admitted softly, but grudgingly. "I think maybe I just haven't run into the right man yet."

Her words might have pierced Zeke to the heart, but he felt deep down that maybe she was still holding back. Sometimes it took confessing the bald truth about yourself to make someone else do the same. "That's pretty much the opposite of how I feel," he said.

"How's that?" Linda asked, her eyes wary.

Zeke carefully put his hand over hers, fearful that too much pressure—or not enough—might send Linda bolting out of his reach. "I found the right woman once."

Linda's eyes widened in surprise.

"My mistake was letting her get away from me."

Slowly, with tantalizing intent, Zeke bent his head closer and closer, and Linda felt her own head tilting up... up to meet him. Her eyes felt misty. Zeke's words struck a chord in her, even if he was just saying them to seduce her. Maybe it was just the way he said them. Or maybe it was that she'd just wanted to hear them so very, very badly.

He looped an arm about her waist and swung her right up to him as his lips touched hers. That old familiar warmth spread quickly through her, the same buzz of excitement, and Linda marveled at how quickly she responded to Zeke. His every move surprised her, yet everything he did seemed right. Perhaps they were just right for each other.

"Mommy and Daddy never kiss for that long," Seth commented from somewhere beside them.

Shocked out of her reverie, Linda glanced down at the twins, who were both staring up at her intently. Even baby Emily let out an interested coo from where she lay, temporarily forsaken, in her carriage.

"I keep forgetting I'm supposed to be a role model or something," Linda said, pushing away slightly.

Zeke's eyes never left her. "You're something, I'll grant you that."

The twins, already bored with adult talk, tore off again, this time deciding they would have a rolling contest. Avoiding eye contact, Zeke and Linda strolled with Emily back to the porch and watched them roll down a short but deep incline in the yard. They were incredibly slow and awkward, but by their squeals and yells someone might have thought they constituted a two-man avalanche.

Linda shook her head, once again thinking about the changes Zeke had brought about in the old house. "I can't believe what you've done here, Zeke. It makes me nostalgic."

But it wasn't just the way he'd changed the house, Linda knew. In a few short days, Zeke had also changed her—again. In the time since they'd last seen each other, she'd found escape in work the way Zeke had found it in travel. Both had reaped rewards. But it was also rewarding to come home and get a reminder of the person you used to be. A person, Linda knew, who was still deep inside her, with all the same yearnings.

Zeke let out one of his short sharp laughs, which in itself brought a smile to Linda's face. "Imagine what it feels like to me. After all, I was the one who grew up here."

"But somehow, it feels like I grew up here, too." At Zeke's puzzled frown, she went on, "I don't know if I can explain it to you. My old house belongs to Naomi now, and her kids. Emily sleeps in my old room. Nothing there belongs to me. But I remember this old house, and how you always wanted it to be. We used to talk about it so much. Now that you've made it over, I sort of feel I had a stake in it, too. I'm glad you fixed it up, Zeke."

He put an arm around her shoulder and pulled her closer. "I never thought I'd move back here. Never."

"And I never thought I'd envy anybody who did," Linda said. "Life here seems so much less intimidating to me now. It's not the traumatic place I remember."

"Not even when you're standing in a basement full of water?" Zeke asked her, amused by her sudden conversion.

"I handled that okay," Linda defended. "Haven't you heard the expression, 'When all else fails, dance'?"

"Not recently," Zeke answered. Then he pulled his arm back and clasped his hands in front of him. It shouldn't be this easy to talk to her, he warned himself. She was so different from him. He cleared his throat. "I guess I seem pretty small-town to you."

"I was afraid I seemed ridiculously citified to you," she said.

"Do you care what I think?" Zeke asked her.

Truth-telling time was at hand, apparently. Linda straightened her back and folded her hands across her lap. To avoid his eyes, she intently studied her knobby fingers. "I guess I do," she confessed. "Call it adult peer pressure."

Zeke would rather have called it something else, but he was holding his breath so that he couldn't have called it anything. The moment was so delicate it seemed that anything his clumsy tongue might come up with would spoil it. He focused on the twins, who were still tumbling noisily down the little hill.

"I can't stop thinking about that game we used to play," Linda said. "I look at Naomi's children and wonder what would have happened if I'd married and had three kids. Or if I'd stayed in Grover's Springs. Would I be happy?"

"Would you be happy here now?" Zeke asked, then immediately wished he hadn't. Her face went blank.

"Under the right circumstances, I might," Linda admitted cautiously. "If I had a reason to be here."

Zeke's heart pumped double-time. "What would be a reason?"

But he knew. They both knew. Responsibilities were the only thing keeping anybody anywhere. It was his responsibility to take care of his father's pitiable legacy that had brought him back, and responsibility to Naomi that kept Linda here for a week. To stay longer, Linda would have to make a choice, which would mean leaving her business behind for more emotional reasons. Maybe even for him. He'd made his own choice.

A low, whirring whine sounded. Zeke looked sharply at Linda's waist, ready to swat away a bug.

"It's my beeper," she said, laughing.

"Oh." Zeke felt a little foolish. He'd seen doctors wearing those things, but he'd never actually heard one go off before. "Your office is calling you?"

"I guess. I'll call when I get home." Linda shrugged with uncharacteristic casualness—for something related to her work, that is. Usually she would have leapt for the nearest phone and knocked down anyone who stood in her way. This time she was reluctant for her idyllic afternoon with Zeke to end. They'd seemed to be on the verge of something. But what?

"I guess I should take you all home now."

Linda feared she'd never find out; but she also feared pursuing the matter further. All this misty-eyed nostalgia was out of character for her. Normally she was a realist. She loved business and technology—yet today, the sight of a tire swing and bed after bed of flowers had knocked a fanciful screw loose in her head. If she wasn't mistaken, she had been on the verge of telling Zeke she would stay in Grover's Springs if he asked her to. But did that even make sense?

Linda Potter had a life of her own. She was a businesswoman, for heaven's sakes, with other businesses depending on her and payrolls to meet. She was a TV-dinner-eating town house dweller and made no apologies for it. Could she really exchange the hum of the hustle-bustle for droning cicadas and remote country living?

"You're right," she announced as she stood forcefully and dusted herself off. "I need to be getting back. I'm sure there are a million things my office needs to ask me." And, more important, a million questions to put to herself.

"Seems they haven't needed you much up till now," Zeke said, observing her change in manner carefully.

Linda pursed her lips. "But Fridays are always tough," she said.

"Okay. C'mon, guys," he hollered at Saul and Seth. "Time to go home."

All the way home, Zeke kicked himself for being such a chump—twice. He'd thought that showing her that house might touch some domestic chord in her, or at least give her a stronger hint of who he was and what his plans were. Maybe his scheme had backfired. Now she seemed more determined to get back to her old life. And since Naomi and William were expected back this evening, Zeke guessed she wouldn't be hanging around much longer.

He'd have to forget her all over again, he thought unhappily, though he still doubted that he'd ever forgotten her to begin with. After their kiss today, he was sure he craved her now more than ever. And he doubted that craving would abate anytime soon.

Chapter Seven

"What do you mean, 'unavoidably detained'?" Linda asked in a meek, frightened voice.

Having received no answer when she called her own home, Naomi had then contacted Jane and asked her to buzz Linda. Now that the communication tag game had come full circle, Linda trembled at the horrible news being delivered. How could Naomi let this happen? Detained for even twenty-four hours meant that she and William would miss the twins' birthday party!

"The car's darn transmission went out," Naomi answered. "I thought that black smoke was probably a bad sign...."

Linda would have used a stronger word than *darn* to describe that transmission. "When?" she asked flatly, wanting to know the worst right off the bat. From the doorway, both the twins and Zeke watched her face anxiously.

"We're shooting to return tomorrow night. Although the man at the shop said the car might be ready by noon," Naomi added optimistically.

Noon! Houston was a four-hour drive. There was no way Naomi and William would make it in time for the party. *No way.* The words kept playing inside her head. No way was she going to get a party ready in time. No way would she survive twenty four- and five-year-olds in the same room. No way.

"If you're worried about the party..."

Linda rolled her eyes. *If?*

"It'll be a cinch."

"Naomi, I haven't even—" She looked over at the twins again, then turned and lowered her voice to a sputtering hiss into the receiver. "Even—even made a cake!"

"No need," Naomi said, in that efficient motherly tone of voice she had. "I ordered a cake from the grocery store."

Thank heavens for that, at least. Linda picked up a pencil and a pad and started scrawling down Naomi's words. Even with Naomi's calm voice giving her instructions, her hand was slippery with nervous sweat.

"Power Rangers?" Linda asked, her voice a panicky whisper. She'd heard of them, but had never bothered to learn what exactly they were. Who'd have thought she'd ever need to know?

"They're in my closet—all you have to do is wrap them."

"But how will I—"

"Believe me, Linda, you'll know a Power Ranger when you see one."

After Naomi had finished giving her the lowdown on the party, Linda felt a tad calmer. It was just a birthday party, after all. No big deal.

"Now put Saul and Seth on the phone," Naomi said.

Linda gestured for Zeke to take Seth into the living room to use the phone in there while Saul stayed with her. When Zeke yelled "Okay!" she handed the phone to her nephew.

While Saul silently listened to his mother, Linda looked shakily at her list of things to do. Tonight she would have to wrap presents, figure out some way to decorate and decide on some activities. Tomorrow she would have to pick up the cake, make the punch and any other refreshments, get the house ready and be ready to receive all those kids by eleven-thirty a.m. If she didn't have a heart attack first!

A horrible thought came to her. What if some mothers refused to leave their children with her? Probably most of them knew her from high school. Who in their right mind would let their children stay with someone they last knew as Wild and Crazy Lindy? Poor Saul and Seth would die if no one came to their party. *She* would die!

As if he had picked up on her thoughts, Saul suddenly let out a pained howl, the likes of which Linda hadn't heard in a full four days. She immediately dashed over. "What's wrong?" she asked Saul, but he could only answer with another piercing yowl.

"What's wrong?" she asked Naomi, snatching the receiver away from her nephew's quivering hands. She put a comforting arm around Saul, and the boy immediately clung to her like a burr.

"He's upset that I won't be there for his birthday party," Naomi explained sadly. Linda could almost hear her sister's voice crack with tension. "Tell him for me that I'll see him as soon as possible."

It saddened Linda to hear Naomi so upset—Naomi, who was always the together one. "Oh, Saul," Linda told her sister's boy, "your mother's coming to see you just as soon as possible. And if she isn't here in time for your party, that'll just mean that your birthday lasts that much longer."

Saul quit trembling quite so hard, gulped in a breath, and looked up at Linda with heartbreaking, teary eyes. "Really?"

Naomi sniffled. "Tell him that his Aunt Linda is going to make this the best birthday he's ever had."

Linda gulped. What was she supposed to say to that? She couldn't very well refuse, especially when Seth was still listening in on the other line. She put a tremulous hand on Saul's shoulder and temporarily blotted that long penciled list of things to do right out of her mind. "I'm going to try to make this the best birthday ever, Saul."

She was rewarded with a huge smile, and then Saul yanked the receiver back into his small hands. "'Bye, Mommy!" he yelled into the phone. Then, unexpectedly, he dropped it and bolted from the room, whooping excitedly. Half a second later Linda could hear Seth joining him.

A minute after she hung up the phone, Zeke appeared in the kitchen doorway, a grin tugging at his lips. "The best birthday ever?"

Linda looked down to discover that she was worrying her thumb—just like Emily! "I don't know where to start," she moaned, sinking into a kitchen chair. "I've got to figure out how to decorate. It just never occurred to me that Naomi wouldn't make it back in time!"

Zeke pulled out a chair and sat next to her. "Need help?"

"Are you kidding?" Linda let out a biting laugh. "I need all the help I can get."

Seth frowned at the crepe paper Linda was twisting together. She was rather pleased with her handiwork, but Saul's big blue eyes were making her jittery. Her nerves were already frayed ragged at the prospect of hostessing this birthday party—which her poor nephews were now expecting to be fabulously successful. Her big question was, what did a smash-up successful party mean to a bunch of five-year-olds?

"Hey, Lindy," Zeke called from behind her. "I think Emily needs taking care of."

She turned abruptly, and saw him holding the baby. He looked so natural standing there with one arm crooked around the tiny child dressed in a sleeper with little pink bunnies all over it. The sight made her want to laugh.

"Okay," she said, getting up and taking the baby from him. She turned to the twins before going upstairs. "You boys have fifteen minutes to play until bedtime." The usual moans and whines followed her announcement.

"Okay, twenty," she said good-naturedly. This was their routine now—they whined and she caved in. Being an aunt had its privileges.

Zeke's footsteps sounded behind her on the stairs. "Lindy?" he asked, hanging back at the doorway to Emily's room.

Linda looked up. God, he was good-looking. No wonder she'd carried a torch for him all these years.

"Are you sure about what you're doing?" he asked. When she didn't answer, he went on. "I mean, it just seems that you're promising these kids an awful lot."

"What do you expect me to do, Zeke?" she asked. "Their mother and father won't be there."

"Just for the party, you said. They'll probably be back tomorrow night."

"Maybe."

"Maybe," Zeke allowed.

"Darn, I forgot the powder. Could you get it from that closet?"

Zeke quickly obliged, handed it to her, and then cleared his throat. "I was, uh, wondering about that sketch you had drawn. You know, the one of the banner you were going to make for the living room."

"What about it?" Linda asked, her nerves once again tightening to a pinch.

"Well, I think it might be better if you made it read 'Happy Birthday, Saul and Seth' instead of 'Happy Birthday, Love Bugs.'"

"Oh." Linda felt her face flame and her shallow confidence evaporating further. She had started using the silly name to establish a sort of rapport—it usually went along with a pre-bedtime tickle fest. But she could see where the twins might not want their pet play name splashed across their living room.

Zeke shrugged. "Even five-year-olds have some dignity, you know."

Linda looked up at him gratefully, then suddenly remembered their kiss—had it only been that afternoon? It seemed like years ago...maybe that was because it had already blended in with her memories of years ago. After a short week, it seemed that Zeke had been right with her, through the past thirteen years, along for the ride.

"Thank heavens you were here during this, Zeke," she told him. "During this whole week. I don't know if I could have handled it myself."

Zeke patted her hand comfortingly. "Sure you could have. Besides, I don't know how much help I'll be from here on out. It's been a while since I was at a birthday party."

She shook her head and finished up with Emily. "Me, too! I think I should consult Jane on this. She'll know what to do."

Five minutes later Linda was once again standing by the phone with notepad in hand.

"Games. You need plenty of games," Jane dictated. "You got that?"

Linda wrote *games* down on her growing list, feeling some relief. Everybody had games! "I believe I can handle that one," she said.

"My sister Brenda's kids always have elaborate birthday parties," Jane said, "but she says you always need something to fall back on until the entertainment arrives."

"Entertainment? You mean I should go rent a video or something?"

"No, the entertainment is the clown." Jane let that little morsel of information dangle over the dead wire before adding, "Or a magician. Brenda says every birthday party has to have a magician or a clown."

Linda's heart stopped. A clown or a magician? This was news to her. "Oh, really?"

Jane responded with a moment of stunned silence before replying. "You don't have a magician or a clown?" Her voice was heavy with foreboding, as if the little party already had a thundercloud hovering over it.

"No," Linda answered in a tiny worried voice. "Do you think I need one?"

She could almost imagine Jane's head shaking slowly back and forth. "Without a magician or a clown, I don't know what you're going to do with twenty little kids for three hours. Pin the Tail on the Donkey will only take you so far."

Linda suddenly thought about those three hours. It hadn't seemed like much this afternoon, when she was trying to keep a stiff upper lip for Naomi's benefit. Now, in the face of Jane's skepticism, the enormity of what she had taken on hit her full force. Three hours. One hundred and eighty minutes. Ten thousand eight hundred seconds. Three long, long hours.

Besides which, Saul and Seth weren't exactly born yesterday. They would know if she had fudged on their big event.

She had to get her hands on a magician or a clown! But where was she going to find either in Grover's Springs?

"Do you really think you need one of those?" Zeke asked when she explained her new dilemma to him later. The twins had been put to bed, and now he was helping cut out the letters for the banner.

"Of course I need a clown!" she cried. "You know how kids are these days. They live and breathe this stuff. It's status."

"Lindy, this is Grover's Springs, not Beverly Hills. Besides, Naomi apparently didn't think it was so important."

Linda let out a tired breath. "Yeah, but Naomi didn't pledge to make this the best birthday ever. I did. Besides, Naomi says things like 'kids practically run themselves.' She's a natural, whereas I'm an impostor in aunt's clothing!''

Already exhausted, with miles yet to go before she slept, Linda flopped dramatically onto the couch.

Zeke laughed and plopped down right beside her. "You're right. It's going to be an unmitigated disaster.''

"Thanks for the vote of confidence." She grabbed a pair of snubbed scissors and began cutting *A*'s. Unfortunately, her mind was working faster than her hands.

"And I've got to find games," she said, suddenly remembering Jane's first rule.

Alarmed, Zeke watched as she darted across the room toward the large closet off the hall.

"We had tons of them growing up," Linda mumbled. She came back into the room with her arms loaded. "Here, look. Monopoly, Pictionary, Scrabble, and we've even got a Ouija board. We might not need a clown at all. We've got games to last a lifetime!''

Zeke didn't like being the one to break the bad news, but somebody had to. "I think you need a clown now more than ever.''

"What are you talking about?" Linda said, dumbfounded. "You were the one who thought I didn't need one.''

"Yeah," Zeke answered wryly, "but that's before I found out that you think five-year-olds could play Scrabble.''

Linda's heart sank. She felt as if she were riding a roller coaster that took her to the dizzying heights of optimism only to plunge her into despair again. All she craved was a nice even keel. "You're right. If they can't spell, they can't play Scrabble. And I doubt I could teach a bunch of preschoolers to enjoy Monopoly.''

"Who does enjoy Monopoly?"

"Are you kidding me?" Linda asked. Then she remembered the last time she'd played. She'd spent three hours bankrupt or in jail. "Well, everybody plays it, anyway."

"Everybody over the age of eight," Zeke conceded. "You must have something in that closet for younger kids."

Linda ducked into the closet once again, but what she saw hardly lifted her spirits. "An Uncle Wiggly game with half the pieces missing and—oh, dear."

"What is it?" Zeke asked, joining her.

"Pin the Tail on the Donkey." Linda shut the door and leaned against it, trying to pull some marvelous party idea out of a hat. If only she *were* a magician!

Zeke came forward and gave her a reassuring hug. "You'll be great," he said encouragingly.

"I wish I could believe that," Linda said.

"Believe it," Zeke said in a quiet voice.

Slowly Linda became aware of a tonal shift in their friendly embrace. When she turned into Zeke's arms, she knew she was playing with dynamite, but for the moment she couldn't quite resist the kind of comfort he was offering. She leaned into his kiss as if it would hold the magic she'd been searching for.

When their lips touched, party anxieties were swept from her mind, and she became completely enveloped in the moment, in the feel of his hand softly caressing her back, in the way their bodies seemed to mesh perfectly together. No wonder she'd never found anyone she'd cared for so much. No wonder...

She resisted the encroaching thoughts for long moments as they continued to touch and taste. And for a moment she even had the tantalizing realization that they were completely alone. The children were asleep. If she and Zeke wanted privacy, they had it—at least until Emily woke up at three....

Zeke stopped the kiss, momentarily resting his forehead against hers. "Lindy..." Was he trying to torture her? Linda wondered. She knew what he was waiting for—the invitation to stay the night that she had just been contemplating extending to him. But she couldn't do that. Not now, when her life was so confusing in so many areas.

"Is something wrong?" Zeke asked.

"I think you'd better leave," Linda said.

Zeke's eyes widened in surprise. "Is it something I said?"

"It's everything! I'm in a panic, Zeke. And the particular kind of comfort you're offering, while tempting, would be a big mistake. Whatever happened to 'just friends'?"

"Maybe that's just not enough for us, Lindy."

Linda took a sharp breath. "I'm hardly in a position to make that decision now, Zeke. It may seem silly to you, but I have a hard task ahead of me tomorrow, and it would be better if you weren't here."

"Why?" Zeke asked. It seemed ludicrous, but he actually looked crushed at not being invited to a preschooler birthday party.

"Because you're a whiz with children, whereas all I can do is whip up business prospectuses and call meetings. I'm good at what I do, Zeke, but I don't know the first thing about kids. So if I'm going to fail—"

"You're not," he assured her.

"But if I'm going to, I don't want you as a witness."

"Not even if I want to be one?" Zeke asked, leaning forward to brush a strand of hair out of her eyes.

"Especially not then," Linda answered. And suddenly she knew with frightening clarity why that was. She cared too much about him to let him see her make a fool of herself. The idea stunned her.

Had she gone and fallen in love with him? Again? It wasn't possible!

"I don't understand," Zeke said, taking her hand. "I thought we were beyond things like that. We seemed to be getting along so well...."

Too well, Linda thought. Zeke was sly that way. His casual, breezy way could sweep her right off her feet and back to Grover's Springs before she ever knew what hit her. Maybe it was just her panic talking, but she didn't think so. She had the sneaking feeling she was already in love with Zeke, and she wasn't sure that was a good thing. Disaster had already visited them once....

Suddenly, Zeke pulled away. "I get it," he said angrily. "I guess some people never learn."

"What?" Heaven knows, she was thinking the same thing, but she couldn't believe she and Zeke were so much in sync that he could read her thoughts that easily.

He rubbed his jaw and his green eyes squinted speculatively into hers. "I had this feeling once before, when I was in the hospital. I watched you walk away, feeling like the boy who'd had the door slammed in his face when he'd asked for too much."

"That's not true!" Linda said, shocked that he was finally bringing up the past now of all times. "That's not even how it happened."

"I waited there a week, Lindy. You never came back."

"I didn't know what to do," Linda argued back. "You acted so cold, like you never wanted to see me again!"

"You didn't even call. Do you know what kind of a fool I felt like?"

Linda shook her head. "You were the one who told me to leave, Zeke."

"So now this time you're telling me," he mused.

"I never—"

The piercing glint in his eye cut her off. With one look, Zeke made her feel raw and exposed. "I thought taking you out to my place might be a mistake, and I guess it was. Scared, that's what you are. Thirteen years ago you couldn't stand up to your father and tell him what you really wanted. I was ready to give you everything I had, paltry as you apparently thought that was." He scathingly looked her up and down. "Now the only person you can't stand up to is yourself."

Before Linda could fully absorb his words, much less respond to them, Zeke quietly turned on his boot heel and strolled out. Out of her life, was what it felt like, and the suddenness of it startled her.

How had things become so confused so quickly? She'd only meant to tell him he couldn't stay the night, but he'd taken it as a flat-out rejection of him. And his wildly surprising take on what happened over a decade before had kept her from setting him straight. The truth in Zeke's words stung, but there was also another side of the story, too. But what did that matter now? For thirteen years they'd both been licking their wounds and holding back from relationships, and neither had truly understood why.

In a daze she returned to the living room to resume her cutting and planning and worrying. All the while Zeke was uppermost in her thoughts, darting in and out, daring her to start forgetting him if she could. But she knew she couldn't. Would he be able to forget her? Suddenly she wanted desperately to run to him, to beg him not to give up on her just yet.

But she couldn't. She used the party preparations as an excuse. But maybe Zeke was right. Maybe she was just plain scared.

When she looked down at the *H* she was cutting, a messy blob, like a starburst, appeared on the red construction paper. Startled, she wiped her eye and inspected her hand. A teardrop, she thought numbly, then tore up the *H* and started again.

After three hours' sleep, a frenzied trip to the grocery store and hours of worry and spastic decorating, Linda had not just one but twenty-one clowns on her hands—twenty preschoolers with painted faces and party hats who were hyper from too much cake and sherbet punch.

Since Grover's Springs wasn't rampant with professional clowns, Linda had spent half the night putting together a clown get-up for herself. She'd settled on a worn pair of William's overalls and his old street shoes, both of which seemed about fifteen sizes too big, a mop wig that made her fear for her head's health and Naomi's floppy garden hat. The result was a pathetic, crazed-looking country clown.

Then, as she stared at the abundance of colors in front of her at Naomi's bureau, she'd been hit with the bright idea of making up all of Saul and Seth's guests into clowns. So all the children had been done up with white flour and huge lipstick smiles and polka dots on their faces. The kids had such a big time with it that Linda was a bit overwhelmed by her success—until devilish little Dooley Turner discovered that terrorizing the little girls with a tube of lipstick was more fun than playing Uncle Wiggly. Then all hell had broken loose.

Only one of the mothers, Mrs. Saunders, had seemed the least bit doubtful about leaving Crazy Lindy the Clown in charge of her child, but in the end, even she had given in to the tempting prospect of having a toddler-free Saturday. In Linda's estimation, Mrs. Saunders's four-year-old, Tubby, was the best behaved of the lot. Of course, at this point her opinion could have been colored by the fact that Tubby was the only one who was actually eating the food instead of throwing it. Tanked up on Twinkies and cake, he joined Linda in watching the chaos around them.

It seemed that every child in Grover's Springs under five was there, making all the noise and creating as much destruction as their tiny frames could manage. Just when she thought all the makeup had been removed from the room, an eyeliner pencil would appear and start a mini-riot, quick and explosive. Linda would run over to break up the excitement, but she was hindered by her too-big shoes and a two-year-old named Carrie, who had been crying for two hours straight and clinging to Linda's baggy leg for almost as long.

Makeup and flour were everywhere. Kids were having a high time crumbling cake down one another's shirts, which eventually worked its way down to the floor. Linda had no idea such little children could create such a big mess!

Unfortunately it was raining cats and dogs, so there was no hope of sending the children outside—and there was still another hour and a half to go before the parents were to start arriving. What was she going to do? Linda especially began to worry when she discovered an anonymous budding artist's masterpiece—a crayon dragon on the wall next to the fireplace. Naomi would kill her... if she managed to survive until Naomi's return!

She dashed to the kitchen for a wet rag and soap. When she returned, a piercing wail sounded through the room, and Linda jumped up to see who it was coming from. The room was a noisy blur, but this particular noise was coming not from the group of children decimating the games, but over behind a chair on the other side of the room.

"Let him go!" she heard one of the twins cry. Since Seth was busy terrorizing a girl with curly blond hair with a mascara tube, the voice had to be Saul's.

With Carrie still attached to her leg, Linda shuffled over to the chair and peeked around it. Saul and another little boy in clown face were entangled on the floor, and somewhere between them, Linda spotted a ball of orange fur that had to be Hippo.

"He's mine!" Saul wailed. "Let him go, Freddy!"

Their legs flailed about as each boy tried to kick the other into letting go of the kitten. Hippo mewed indignantly at being caught in the middle of such a tussle.

"Boys!" Linda hollered above the din in the room. Perspiring nervously, she whipped the mop off her head and swiped a hand through her damp hair. "Let the kitten go."

She bodily brought both boys to their feet. Saul clung protectively to Hippo. Beneath its dusting of flour, his small face was beet red, and when Linda tried to take the kitten from him, he jerked away.

"Saul," Linda said in what she hoped was a patient voice, "do you remember my telling you that Hippo couldn't come to the birthday party?"

Saul nodded, but he still didn't give the kitten to her. "He's not hurting anybody," he argued. "Nobody even knew we were over here till Freddy came and bugged us.''

Guilt stabbed at Linda. She certainly hadn't noticed that Saul had been hiding with his kitten. The shy boy had probably retreated to the corner sometime before the makeup crisis. She sympathized with his desire to be alone, but she felt she ought to make some effort to help him join the group. Saul would never mingle with the other kids when his kitten was there to fall back on.

"Saul, you have to entertain your guests," Linda explained. "And you wouldn't want Hippo to get hurt from too much attention, would you?"

"Hippo!" Seth cried from across the room.

Uh-oh. A wave of dread hit Linda as she heard Seth come running over, and then the thunder of little feet following him.

"A kitten!" squealed one of the girls, and several children echoed her cry.

In that instant Linda read a panicky fear in Saul's eyes that was surely mirrored in her own. She reached for the kitten, which Saul gave up without argument this time. When she turned around, she knew why—she was surrounded by eager, grabby clowns dying to touch the kitten.

"You said we couldn't bring Hippopotamus to the party!" Seth argued.

"I'm taking him to his porch right now," Linda replied, but as she attempted to break free from the circle of bodies that had her pinned against the chair, cries of protest went up.

"I wanna hold it!"

"Me, too!"

"It's mine!"

With one hand clutching Hippo and the other braced against the chair for support, Linda prepared to do battle to get to the nearest door. Everywhere she turned, hands were grabbing at her, and the kitten, understandably frightened, dug its claws into her upper arm.

"Ouch!" she cried when the sharp nails punctured her skin. Before she knew what was happening, Hippo had made a break for it and was leaping toward a bookshelf. Instinctively she reached for the kitten, but was thrown off balance by Carrie, who had anxiously grabbed both of her legs during the excitement.

With amazement, she felt herself topple over as if in slow motion. She began to flap her arms like a chicken in an attempt to defy the gravity that was pulling her down, down, ever closer to those small faces. Half of them were focused on her; the more unobservant ones were still looking at the cat. Before she collided with the hard floor, Linda saw that Hippo at least had made it to safety.

She landed rump first on the old Persian carpet. The room quieted immediately. Something tugged at her sleeve and she turned. At eye level, Saul's face seemed larger than normal. Worry was etched in his brow.

"Are you okay, Aunt Lindy?" the boy asked.

Okay? Linda wondered for a moment. Physically, she was okay—for now—but how was she going to survive for another hour and a half?

"Lindy the clown fell down," came a little girl's voice from the back of the group.

The pronouncement was met with muffled giggles. Seeing her only slim opportunity to save face, Linda forced her lipsticked mouth up into a sickly clown smile. "She's a poet and didn't know it!" she cried inanely.

Nevertheless, the kids loved it. Or maybe they were just relieved that the so-called adult in the room wasn't going to have a nervous breakdown after all. Either way, their laughter went a long way in lifting Linda's spirits.

"Lindy the clown fell down!" one of the boys chanted, and several other children followed suit.

Linda was grateful to hear the room return to its customary uproar, and immediately turned to the important job of dragon erasing. So involved in this task did she become that she failed to notice someone new entering the house until at least half the children let out a gigantic whoop.

When she jerked her head up, she was stunned to be staring into the eyes of a six-foot clown bearing pizzas.

Chapter Eight

Zeke finally pulled his attention away from the multitude of tiny white faces long enough to catch sight of Linda kneeling on the floor amidst the room's chaos. What was that outfit she'd cooked up? He was glad she didn't appear to be as indignant as he had expected at his waltzing in at the eleventh hour—and the wary warmth in her eyes held definite promise of forgiveness for the way he'd walked out on her the night before.

"Zeke!" she cried, standing and coming forward in her crazy big shoes. A little girl clinging to her leg moved in lockstep with her.

Suddenly Zeke remembered his own bizarre appearance. "I seem to be right in style," he told Linda as she relieved him of a pizza box.

She smirked. "I see you went for more of a straight Bozo effect," she said, giving his multicolored wig and checked overalls an approving once-over. "Not very original, but I like it."

"Believe it or not, it belongs to George." The store-keeper had reluctantly produced it from a dusty chest in his attic when Zeke told him of his dilemma. Halloween 1974, the older man had explained grimly.

"You're right, I don't believe it," Linda said, then broke into a laugh. She couldn't even imagine George Warren in this outfit. Maybe she didn't know the old crank as well as she thought she did.

"How about we tear into these pizzas, guys," Zeke suggested to the children, who hollered and jumped and followed him to the table. He shoved back the uneaten cake to make way for the pizza boxes, and Linda appeared at his side to dispense the new round of food and drink to the kids.

"Thank goodness you brought something resembling real food," she said.

"I figured they'd be jittery from all that sugar," Zeke remarked. "This'll help calm them down."

"I'm so glad you walked through that door," Lindy suddenly admitted in a rush. She looked up at him with gratefulness in her beautiful gray eyes.

"Why? It looked like the party was going great guns to me."

"Yeah . . . but take a gander at the room—it's a disaster area, and I was out of ideas for what to do with the rest of the afternoon."

Zeke playfully ruffled her frazzled hair, and Linda was suddenly joyful that she'd already discarded the yucky mop. "Don't sell yourself short," he told her. "I walked into a roomful of happy kids just now."

"Didn't you have to work at the Bledsoes' today?" she asked, pouring a cup of punch.

He nodded in the direction of the window. "I couldn't work on the roof in the rain."

"Oh."

"Would you rather I said that I simply couldn't stay away a moment longer?" Zeke asked jokingly.

"No, it's just that a few minutes ago I was cursing the rain. But because of it you were able to save my neck."

"Pretty neck," Zeke said with a wink.

Linda rolled her eyes. "I plan to pay you for all of this, of course."

"I intend to let you."

She looked at him suspiciously.

"Dinner?" he asked.

"Cash," she answered adamantly.

"Cash, then," Zeke agreed, crossing his arms. "And I'll throw in a story in return for dinner."

"Yeah, a story!" Seth cried, and several others chimed in.

"Zeke tells the best stories," Saul explained, as if he personally owned this new clown.

Linda handed a plate down and couldn't help admitting to Zeke, "When you walked out last night I thought I'd never see you again."

"Disappointed?"

She laughed. "Frankly, I would have been glad to see any other adult today."

"Cagey to the end," Zeke said with a dramatic sigh.

Linda laughed. "I have to be, with you hanging around all the time."

But personal matters had to be put on hold. Five minutes later Zeke was seated on the couch with kids piled all around him, eating their pizza and listening to the story of Walter the Wildebeast, who had the hots for a wildebeast chick named Wilma.

Linda worried what the parents of these children would think when they heard about Walter around their dinner tables this evening. But the children themselves apparently thought nothing of it. They kept on munching. Actually, they appeared to like the story more when Walter went on his quest for food. There was a drought, and he hoped to impress Wilma by finding pizza for all the little wildebeast children.

Obviously Zeke intended to milk his heroism for all it was worth. And Linda had to admit, he was her hero for the day. In fact, he was the hero for the entire week.

And just perhaps, she thought, trying to gauge the snappy little feeling just looking into those green eyes caused, perhaps he was her hero for life. Maybe he was her one special man that every woman was fated to find in life. Even in green-checked pants and a shiny red bulbous clown nose, he charmed the socks off her. It had to be love.

But Zeke hadn't mentioned anything about love...or anything else. And all he'd brought up about the past was the bitterness he still felt. That certainly wasn't much to forge a relationship on.

But he hadn't mentioned any relationship, she reminded herself again. He hadn't done anything except make her fall in love with him. Damn, she thought angrily. Zeke could snare her affection as easily as he was able to capture children's attention. How did he do it? And what was she going to do about it?

She couldn't imagine keeping up a long-distance relationship with Zeke, and she certainly didn't see herself abandoning her business and moving in with Naomi and William for the summer just so she could carry on with the town's favorite handyman. But equally unimaginable was the image of Zeke living happily in a little Dallas town house.

The situation was untenable. There was no way a further relationship between them could work. So why was her mind racing with ideas to make it work? The image of Seth trying to pound the wrong piece of a jigsaw puzzle into place with his fist came to mind. Was that what she was trying to do?

Linda hadn't been aware that she was even listening to the story, but when Walter and Wilma wound up giving each other an icky slurpy kiss at the altar, she found herself moaning and applauding with the rest of the audience. And when Zeke's gaze zoomed in on her, that little happy buzz zipped through her once again. He made her believe in happily-ever-after, too.

Hours later, after the last mother had retrieved her child and most remnants of the party were gone, Zeke stood next to Linda at the sink, drying the dishes she handed to him. The tedious work was made all the more unbearable—and irresistible—by the fine edge of tension between them. He tried to keep his distance from her, to give her space, but they seemed to gravitate toward each other. Then, with each accidental touch of fingers or rubbing of shoulders, they would each jump back to their original places.

Linda, who like Zeke was freshly showered and wearing jeans and a T-shirt, was especially disturbed by the sudden silence around them. After the ruckus of the party, it seemed almost eerie. There was nothing to concentrate on but the man standing next to her, and she feared where that would lead. They still had some important things to talk through, but mostly all she could think about was how glad she was that he was there.

Just when she was drying one of the last punch cups, when she was almost certain her nerves were strung as tightly as they could be, the doorbell rang.

"Who could that be?" she asked, jerking her head nervously toward the sound.

Zeke shrugged. "Do you think we missed a kid somewhere?"

Linda put down her drying towel and started for the door. "No, I think we managed to foist them all off on their parents."

She was still smiling as she swung open the door, but when she saw what was on the other side, her smile froze. A large lunk of a man, soaking wet in a pink clown suit, towered over them.

"So," he asked nonchalantly, "did I miss the party?" He stared sullenly over her and Zeke's shoulders as if dreading to see a roomful of children awaiting his arrival.

"Who are you?" Linda asked.

The man's big red-and-pink mouth turned down in an offended pout. It was then that Linda noticed he was carrying a basket loaded with bubble gum under one arm. "Hey, lady, you booked me," he snapped out. "I'm Bubba the Bubble Gum Clown, remember?"

"Oh..." Somehow, Linda knew that laughing would be the wrong thing to do at this precise moment.

"Listen," the disgruntled clown continued, spurred on by her silence, "do you think I wanted it to rain? Do you think I wanted my clunker of a car to break down between Shreveport and here? I mean, excuse me, but clowns don't get paid enough in this country to run around in Cadillacs, you know."

Linda didn't know how she was going to respond—or even if she would be able to—until she felt Zeke gently pinch her arm. "I'm sorry, Mr. . . . uh, Bubba," she managed to spit out finally. "We've had a rather bad day also, but I'm afraid you've missed the party."

"That's too bad," he said flatly. Then he held out his basket to them. "The bubble gum's yours to keep."

"Oh, but we don't—"

"You might as well take it, because I can't give you back the deposit," he insisted. "I had to use it for gas. Lot of good it did me."

With that, he plopped the basket down on the porch, turned and stomped back to his old clunker. The car was a vintage, late-seventies sedan, and from the looks of it, Linda had a hunch that clown might never make it back to Shreveport. Especially when it set off down Sycamore Street with a chug and a roar.

She slowly shut the door, then turned to Zeke. All at once both of them let out their pent-up nerves in a burst of mirth. Zeke was practically doubled over, and Linda laughed until her jaws began to ache.

"Maybe it's a good thing he didn't make it to the party," she finally managed to say.

"I don't know," Zeke said, sobering, "what's another clown, more or less?"

"Even a cranky one?"

They started walking back to the kitchen but were interrupted by Saul.

"Aunt Lindy?"

"What is it?" she asked, straining to keep her voice measured. If he'd been watching, he probably thought they were both crazy.

"Hippo's gone."

"Gone?" Linda was alarmed. "Where?"

She could have kicked herself for asking such a stupid question. Obviously the child didn't know, and that fact became more obvious when tears started streaming down his face. He shook his head miserably.

Zeke walked over to Saul and patted him on the shoulder. "Don't worry, Saul," he said. "Hippopotamus will come back."

"I don't think so," Saul said between gasping sobs.

"Why not?" Linda asked.

"'Cause I threw him over the fence."

Linda and Zeke exchanged startled looks. If she lived to be a hundred, Linda wondered if she would ever understand kids. Just hours ago Saul was clinging to that cat as if it were his best friend in the world; now apparently he had expelled him from the house.

"Why did you do that, Saul?" Zeke asked.

"I didn't want the other kids to get him."

His explanation made perfect sense to Linda. She had been worried about the same thing herself. That's why she had banned the kitty from the birthday party in the first place.

"Did you put him out in the yard?" she asked.

Saul shook his head, creating a gnawing fear in Linda. She tried to remain calm. "Where did you take him?"

"Down the street."

"Where to?" Zeke asked, kneeling.

The boy's nerves finally cracked under the inquisition. Saul's teary eyes looked into Zeke's. "I don't remember!" he exclaimed, and then he ran from the room.

Zeke squared his shoulders and stood up. "What now?"

Linda stared at him unbelievingly. "I should think that would be perfectly obvious. We have to find Hippo."

She walked briskly to the hall closet and grabbed a jacket and a flashlight. "Aren't you coming?" she asked Zeke, who was still standing in the same place.

He pointed to her flashlight skeptically. "Do you really think you'll need that? It's not even dark yet."

"It might be by the time we find Hippo," Linda replied crisply. "Or maybe he ran under someone's house." She was surprised at how panicked she was at the idea of Hippo out loose in the world. She guessed that sometime in the past week she must have bonded with that little fur ball. Or probably, it was her new bond with Hippo's owners that most concerned her.

"I was just wondering if we should use my truck to look for him," Zeke said thoughtfully.

"On foot," Linda said. She spotted Saul, lying in a miserable ball in the corner of the dining room. "Could you put a jacket on him while I get the other two?" she asked Zeke. She gestured toward the front hall closet and headed for the staircase.

"Aunt Lindy?" Saul's meek voice sounded behind her. Linda turned.

"I forgot to tell you . . . Seth's gone, too."

Zeke would never forget the terrible paleness that came over Lindy in the matter of a split second, or the raw fear in her shock-widened eyes. But in a moment she set her jaw forward and nodded tersely. Turning her attention to him, she said simply, "We'll need to bring the extra jacket along."

"Seth!"

"Here, kitty kitty!"

"Seth!"

The sounds of Zeke's, Linda's and occasionally Saul's voices echoed down Sycamore Street. The rain had stopped, leaving a slippery, dewy, muddy mess for their search in the foggy afternoon light. This was not a good time to have lost a cat or a child, Linda thought helplessly.

Apparently, when Seth had found Hippo missing—which, as near as Zeke and Linda could tell, must have been a while after Saul had let the kitten go—the boy had set out on his own to hunt for it. Piecing the story together was difficult because Saul was repentant and hysterical by turns.

Neighbors, some of whom had been sitting on their porches, came up to their fence lines to ask what had happened.

"Lost one of Naomi's kids, did ya?" old Mr. Peterson asked. The way he was shaking his head made Linda think that he had expected this to happen someday.

"And a cat," Saul supplied helpfully.

The old man shook his head some more and returned to his porch. Linda's morale was about as low as it could get, but what was worse, she was quivering with fear. What would she say to Naomi if, God forbid, something happened? The thought made her feel physically ill.

"Don't worry," Zeke said as they passed the Jenkins house, both of them peering up at the trees and through the shrubs that lined the place. "We'll find him."

"I should call the police."

"We'll find him," Zeke repeated.

But Linda wasn't so sure. After all, when she had run away, she had gone all the way to Waco. No one would have found her there—if she hadn't called home, that is. The rational part of her kept telling her that Seth hadn't run away, exactly, as much as he had simply gone on an errand. Nor was he seventeen.

"He went by this way 'bout fifteen minutes ago," Ed Jenkins offered, coming out to the sidewalk to greet them.

"Seth did?" Linda asked, her heart racing frantically.

"One of them," the man replied, peering at Saul beside them. "I'm not sure which."

Linda could have hugged the old man, and she made a mental note not to hold the time he had refused to let his son Frank take her to a high school dance against him anymore.

"Don't worry too much, you'll find him," Mr. Jenkins said, giving her an encouraging pat on the arm. Then he chuckled. "I used to lose one or another of my kids every month or so. They never went far."

"Thank you, Mr. Jenkins," she said sincerely. The man had just won himself a full pardon in her esteem.

"Sure thing," he answered.

"There, you see?" Zeke said when they were a little farther down the sidewalk. "We'll find him."

Linda, even as she diligently looked for Seth, was still amazed at how helpful Mr. Jenkins had been.

"I saw one of Naomi's little boys just a few minutes ago," Caroline Ford informed them a few minutes later. She had been sitting on her porch enjoying the end of the rain, too, so it was natural that she would have seen Seth. "He kept walking up and down the sidewalk. Then he turned in at Vera's." The woman motioned two houses back up the street and took a moment to tweak little Emily's cheek in her stroller.

As glad as Linda was to hear that her nephew had returned to their next-door neighbor's, the mere mention of Vera Huckabee's name sent a stab of dread through her. "Mrs. Huckabee?" she asked.

"That's right. He looked like he was headed for her backyard."

Linda forced a wan smile. "Thank you so much," she said to Mrs. Ford, then continued on more slowly. Leave it to Seth to force her to enter the lion's den to rescue him.

Sure enough, as they stopped in front of Mrs. Huckabee's, they could just glimpse the corner of Seth's shirt through the wood slats of the fence that divided the woman's front and back yards. Linda gave Mrs. Huckabee's well-manicured pansy beds a quick once-over and winced. The ones in the backyard were even more elaborate.

As soon as he saw his brother, Saul broke loose from Zeke and ran toward him. Seth was standing with his small fists planted on his hips, staring up into the branches of a large oak. Or at least he was until, in a rush of relief, Linda left Emily's stroller with Zeke and ran to her nephew. She picked him up and hugged him until she was worried neither would be able to breathe.

"I was so scared!" she told Seth, barely keeping her tears in check.

"Uh-oh," Zeke murmured as he pulled Emily's stroller up beside her. "Cat's in the tree."

"Up there," Seth said, pointing to the high branches.

"Oh, no." Linda's reaction wasn't so much to the news about Hippo as it was to the sight of Mrs. Huckabee standing on the other side of the tree, sending her a pursed-lipped frown.

If she could have turned around and run back up Sycamore Street to Naomi's, she would have. But she couldn't. Seth and Saul weren't going to leave that yard until their kitten was out of the tree. She had to get that cat down, fast. Taking a deep breath, she stepped forward to face Mrs. Huckabee.

"Looks like you misplaced something," Vera said in her slightly scratchy voice. As Linda became calmer, she could also hear the kitten's desperate mewing. Funny, but it sounded as if Hippo were meowing in stereo. She looked up. The kitten was perched on a skinny branch high up in the tree. Way, way high up.

"A couple of things," Linda amended, referring to Seth. She might as well own up to her mistakes; Vera Huckabee would point them out, anyway. She clung all the more tightly to her nephew. Now she knew what *worried sick* truly meant.

"I had to find Hippopotamus," Seth explained, unrepentant.

"Cat's in the tree," Mrs. Huckabee said.

"Mmm."

"Found that boy in one of my flower beds, yelling up at the animal."

Linda gritted her teeth and responded, "I hope he didn't do too much damage." *If she dared start grousing about those flower beds* . . .

But Mrs. Huckabee shook her head. "Nope, I found him fast enough." To Linda's shock, the older woman looked at her sideways and said, "I can remember another child who was fond of wandering. I don't wonder who this boy takes after!"

In shock, Linda smiled lamely and they all stood in silence for a moment, staring at the impossibly thick trunk of the oak. The first branch of the old tree was many feet higher up than any of them could reach, with the possible exception of Zeke, if he stood on a ladder.

"I'll have to go get my truck," Zeke said.

Contemplating backing a pickup into the yard under Mrs. Huckabee's disapproving stare, Linda blurted out, "Shouldn't we just call the fire department? Don't they specialize in this type of thing?"

Mrs. Huckabee frowned. "It's obvious you don't pay taxes here, Lindy Potter. That would be a terrible waste of their time."

Linda's shoulders sagged a little and Zeke gave her a pat on the shoulder. "I'll only be gone for a few minutes. I just need to get my ladder."

"Oh!" Mrs. Huckabee beamed at him. "I have a ladder. It's in the garage."

Zeke loped over to get it, and Linda again peered up into the tree. "I could swear I hear *two* cats." She listened again and heard the strange echo of Hippo's plaintive meow and turned back to Mrs. Huckabee. "Did you hear that?"

"Hear what?"

Linda wondered for a second whether one of the twins was playing tricks on her. But when she looked down at them, they also were staring at her as if she'd gone bonkers. "I guess I'm just going crazy," she muttered.

Zeke came back hauling a tall metal ladder and leaned it against the tree. Linda made a move toward it, but he stopped her with a hand to her shoulder. "I'll go. You're shaky enough on stairs."

Linda smiled and stepped back, glad not to have to go up. She'd never liked heights.

Mrs. Huckabee didn't miss a beat. Once Zeke was out of earshot, she asked, "So, have you to decided to stay with us, Lindy?"

"Me?" Linda asked. In Grover's Springs? It seemed preposterous put so baldly. But as she watched Zeke groping around in the branches overhead, she realized she still didn't know what the answer to that question was. Not yet.

"Well, anyhow, you shouldn't be such a stranger. Town's been dead without you, you know." She paused for a moment. "And now, old George Warren can't stop talking about your miniskirt. Looks like I'm gonna have to get myself one of those infernal things."

Linda stared at her neighbor, slack-jawed. Had the woman gone insane? But no, Mrs. Huckabee was standing with her arms crossed casually, looking up at Zeke, too. "Goodness, he sure is high up," Vera said.

Linda shook her head. Maybe small towns didn't remember as well as she'd assumed. Or maybe they were more forgiving than she gave them credit for.

"Uh-oh," Zeke said.

Oh, no, Linda thought. If anything had happened to that kitten, she'd never forgive herself. The twins probably wouldn't forgive her, either.

"What is it?" she asked.

Zeke quickly came down the ladder and handed her a ball of fur. "It's an impostor. Hippo is still up there."

The kitten, which was as small as Hippo and able to fit in the palm of Zeke's hand, stared calmly up at Linda. Its tiger markings made it a duplicate of Saul and Seth's kitty, except it had a black mark that looked like a Rorschach test on its nose.

"Goodness, I wonder where that came from!" Mrs. Huckabee exclaimed. To Linda's mind, the kitten's answering meow to the elderly lady's voice was suspiciously familiar—as if that kitten knew exactly who Mrs. Huckabee was. And her suspicions grew by leaps and bounds when a mama tiger cat suddenly appeared at Vera Huckabee's feet, purring lovingly against her leg.

"I want it!" Saul exclaimed, reaching up for the kitten.

"It's Hippo's brother!" Seth said.

"Can we keep it, Aunt Lindy?"

Oh, no, Linda thought, *not again.* "Your mother will be back soon..." She shrugged helplessly as the child took the cat from her and Zeke climbed up to save Hippo.

"He seems like an awfully nice kitten," Mrs. Huckabee said confidentially.

Linda looked thoughtfully at the older woman, then looked down at the big cat at the woman's feet. "I'd think you would consider keeping it, since you love cats."

"Me?" Vera Huckabee asked innocently. "I'm full up."

Right, Linda thought. But probably less "full up" than she was before she'd foisted off two kittens on her visiting next-door neighbor.

"And you always loved animals so," Vera continued. "I'm sure you can talk Naomi into doing the right thing."

So. Vera's visit with the brownies hadn't been to spy on her and Zeke at all, probably. The woman most likely just wanted to make sure Hippo had landed on his target. Linda suppressed a laugh. She and Zeke had argued after that innocent visit—over nothing, apparently.

"Got him," Zeke announced from above. "Safe and sound."

Linda breathed a sigh of relief. Now if only Zeke would get off that darn ladder, her heartbeat might return to normal for the first time in about twenty-four hours.

"Uh-oh," Zeke said.

Linda squinted up into the branches. Not another kitten! Did Mrs. Huckabee expect Emily to adopt one, too? "What is it?" she asked, not really wanting to know the answer.

"Car coming in next door."

Linda stiffened, then shot a glance toward the thick hedge that separated the properties. It was too soon, she thought anxiously. She wasn't ready. The house was still a mess from the party, the twins would be in an uproar about the kittens, and...Zeke. How was she going to explain Zeke to Naomi? And what exactly was there to explain?

Maybe he was wrong, she thought, straining to see over the hedge. Maybe someone was just using the hedge to turn around....

"It's a station wagon," Zeke observed, dashing her hopes. "Your sister's back."

Funny, Linda thought. All week long she would have given her right arm to see that station wagon pulling up. Now she had mixed feelings. Mommy duty was over... but so was her reason for being in Grover's Springs.

Chapter Nine

"Two kittens?"

Linda grimaced under Naomi's not-so-amused stare and held her coffee cup with a steely grip. "It was that Vera Huckabee—"

Naomi laughed. "Are you two still at war?"

"As a matter of fact, no. But that's because we're both animal lovers, I think. And I can vouch for those cats, Naomi. They're really sweet."

"Hmm." In the ensuing silence, Naomi tapped her fingers against the kitchen tabletop. William was upstairs getting the twins ready for bed, Emily was already put down, and Linda was nervous. After dinner they had talked about the party, the kids, and the clown that Naomi had neglected to warn Linda about. Now that they were alone, she didn't know what she was going to say if Naomi asked her about herself.

But sure enough, she did.

"So... wasn't that Zeke Howell with you as we drove up?"

"That was your fault," Linda defended. "*He* was the one George Warren sent over."

Linda had spent the entire evening preoccupied with what would happen next. Had Naomi's arrival put the kibosh on Zeke's attention to her? Would she see him again? Should she return to Dallas tomorrow and hope he would contact her?

"I expected him to fix the washing machine, Linda," Naomi admonished, "not sweep you off your feet."

Had he done that? Suddenly Linda remembered the feeling of being airborne when she'd slipped on Seth's toy car. Then that sensation seemed to blend in with the robust swinging she'd done in Zeke's backyard yesterday afternoon. It seemed she'd somehow been up in the air and off balance since seeing Zeke again. *Something* had swept her off her feet!

"Linda?"

She looked up into Naomi's worried face. "Are you okay?"

Linda blinked. "Why?"

"You were laughing to yourself." Her sister's lips were pursed in a frown.

"I was?" Linda laughed again. "I guess I was...."

Somewhere in the back of her mind—or maybe it was just far off—she heard a whistle. That old familiar whistle. Her head darted around toward the back door.

"Linda?" Naomi asked. "Linda, you're acting awfully funny tonight. Are you sure you're okay?"

The whistle sounded again, coming from down the street. Instinctively Linda hopped out of her chair. "I've got to go!" she told Naomi.

"*Now?* But it's dark. Where?"

"Don't worry, I'll be back in an hour or so. I'm just going for a walk!"

Before her sister could interrogate her further—and before Linda could think too much about what she was doing—she flew out the door and hit the sidewalk running. This was silly! She felt like a kid, like a giddy teenager again. But that was how Zeke made her feel. Giddy.

Someday soon, she knew, she was going to have to think about where all this was leading. She just couldn't jump to Zeke's whistle forever—or for even another week, probably. Someday she would have to come to terms with who she and Zeke had become, and where they were going.

Someday.

Right now she didn't feel like thinking beyond how her heart thrilled to see him standing at the wrought-iron gates marking the entrance of the Cornelius Grover Municipal Park. As she came closer, she saw that old familiar smile form on his lips, revealing those straight white teeth gleaming in the moonlight. He was one sexy man.

"I thought you might not come," he said, taking her hand right away. They walked side by side into the park. "I know I should have come to the door—"

"No," Linda corrected. Zeke raised one alarmed eyebrow, and she hastened to explain. "I needed to get out of there. Do you realize this is the first time we've been alone all week?"

"That's what happens when you have kids."

Linda laughed. "We've been having to cope with a lot of married-couple stuff, haven't we?"

A little surge of hopefulness took its place in Zeke's heart. He wondered what Lindy would think if he came out and said what was actually on his mind—that he wouldn't mind if they actually *were* a married couple.

But he didn't say it, because he was afraid of rushing her. Instead of risking too much at once, he kept his hopes to himself and tried to keep the mood light. He didn't want to frighten her away.

"Hey, look where we are," he said.

"The park?" Linda glanced around at the unassuming park, which occupied a small city block. Aside from the fountain, which stood smack-dab in the center, the only other amenities the space boasted were the jungle gym, slide and swing set on the opposite side. Right now, they had the park to themselves.

"Remember what happened the last time we were together here at night?"

In spite of the darkness, Linda found her gaze glued to the unlit fountain, remembering. She remembered— even though she had spent a good deal of time in the past thirteen years trying to forget her one and only arrest. "I guess it's a good thing we've both grown up."

Zeke shrugged. "I suppose being old and stuffy is better than being young and foolish."

"And in jail."

"That, too," he allowed. They kept strolling along the sidewalk toward the Cornelius Grover fountain.

Linda had the prickly feeling that she should avoid that fountain. Well, she rationalized, there was only one sidewalk and that's where it led. She hadn't planned the park's layout. "I wouldn't describe myself as old and stuffy," she said, then cast Zeke a sideways glance. "Would you?"

"No, no," he said. "Well . . ."

"What? I'm only thirty!" she defended.

"I was thinking about the stuffy part."

"Who, me?" Linda couldn't help being a little offended. "And don't give me that you're-not-the-girl-I-used-to-know routine, either, Zeke Howell, because I'll grant you that."

"True, you're not a girl anymore."

"That's right," she agreed, then stopped in her tracks and glared at him accusingly. "What's that supposed to mean?"

Zeke smiled, then took her other hand in his and gave her a leisurely once-over at arm's length. "I mean, you've become some kind of woman, Lindy Potter."

"Oh." Linda felt herself blush furiously and tugged her hands away from his. She continued walking. "But I still say I'm not stuffy."

Undaunted, Zeke kept pace with her. "Just all business, I guess," he said casually.

But Linda caught the slightest hint of challenge in those words. "That's not true! I've hardly thought about my business this whole week."

"Then what's a fax machine doing in your sister's living room?"

"That was a precaution, in case my office needed me. It's not even hooked up."

They finally reached the fountain, which was really just a statue of a Victorian-looking man standing in the center of a round pool of tepid water. A few jets burbled along the rim, refilling the water supply—or mulling it around a little. It wasn't much as far as fountains went, but Zeke was glad to sit on its ledge and take a load off.

"Still," he said as he stretched out his legs, "I think I liked you best when you were sloshing around with the boys in Naomi's basement. There's just something about you and water...."

"Very funny," Linda answered. Without thinking she pushed off her shoes and sat next to him and began rolling up the cuffs of her jeans. Though only June, the evening was hot enough for July; plus the rain had made the air sticky. It would feel great to soak even her feet.

"Water seems to bring out the exhibitionist in you," Zeke said, noting her bare feet curiously. "Nice toenail polish."

Linda inspected her hot-pink toenails critically. "The fuchsia was supposed to match my sandals."

"Tell me," Zeke asked as Linda stood and began wading around in the fountain. "When you're at work and wearing those suits and pumps, are you always harboring crazy-colored toenails?"

Linda laughed. "Okay, you've discovered the big secret. My wild streak's been relegated to my toenails."

"But not on your day off," Zeke countered, loving to see her loosen up.

"No," she agreed, "and not on vacation. This feels good, by the way."

"Looks like it," Zeke agreed. "So what was that song you sang that night that the police got so wound up?"

"'Girls Just Wanna Have Fun.' Stupid song. I don't listen to that stuff anymore. I'm into oldies now."

Zeke stared at her disbelievingly. "*You?* How old is oldies?"

"Like, I don't know, Gershwin. Have you ever heard this one?" She sang a few warbly but heartfelt lines of "Beginner's Luck."

Zeke laughed and joined her on the refrain. And then they both had to stop for laughing at the sound of his deep baritone belting out the silly phrase. "I don't know where I picked that up, though."

"Probably on the late show. It's an old number Fred Astaire sang."

"I don't remember," Zeke said.

"You must," Linda insisted. "It's in *Shall We Dance,* when he and Ginger are on the boat."

"Doesn't ring a bell."

Linda threw up her hands in disgust. "They're standing at the railing, and Ginger's holding her little dog, and Fred sings the song to her. You know." She started singing again.

And she was off. Zeke leaned back on his elbows to enjoy the floor show as Lindy proceeded to act out the parts of both Fred *and* Ginger, which required her to do quite a bit of sloshing back and forth. At one point she splashed water on Zeke and he splashed her back. Without missing a beat, she continued her chirpy song and kicked water his way. In no time they were in the middle of an all-out water war, accompanied by Lindy imitating Fred wooing Ginger.

And before they knew it, they saw flashing lights coming down the street toward the park.

"Oh, no," Linda moaned. She actually thought for a moment of taking off in a run, but the policeman was already getting out of his car. Naturally, it was Dwight Doggett, looking about as happy as a man could be.

"Hey, now!" he said, coming upon the scene of the crime.

Linda and Zeke still stood in the shin-high water, resigned to what was surely coming next. Only in Grover's Springs, Linda thought, would a police officer begin an arrest with the words "Hey, now."

"I am so sorry!" Linda moaned for what had to be the hundredth time. Then she sneezed.

Zeke bit back a smile, though Linda couldn't see him over the sheet Dwight Doggett had rigged up. Usually the two facing cells sat empty, but on the rare occasion when both were occupied by different sexes, propriety demanded some form of official separation.

"I told you not to get upset," he said, adding wryly, "you'd think you'd never been in jail before."

"Oh, don't joke!" Linda felt miserable—and not only because she found the air-conditioned jail cold and clammy in her wet clothes. She couldn't believe she'd actually landed Zeke in the one place he'd always prided himself in staying away from, except when he'd had to bail out his poor father. This place must carry a terrible burden of memory for him. Just thinking about it made her feel completely ashamed. "I don't know how I'm going to explain this to Naomi."

"Tell her taking care of those kids all week made you go a little haywire."

"It must have," Linda said, wrapping the city-issue blanket more tightly around her shoulders. Her teeth were chattering. "Otherwise, what was I thinking? Fred Astaire didn't even dance in that number!"

"Hey, Zeke," Dwight Doggett interrupted. The officer, who had just hung up the phone, had his feet propped up on his desk in a rather unofficial-looking way. "I just spoke with George. He's coming to bail you out."

"I don't see why Zeke should even be here," Linda argued with the man, who she couldn't even see. "*I* was the one making the public disturbance, if you could call it that. Can't people sing in Grover's Springs anymore?"

"We had a complaint, and you two were caught red-handed." He chuckled long and loud. "Yes, sir, just like last time." More chuckles.

Linda thought she would scream. "Except last time I had youth as an excuse," she said with a groan.

As if she wasn't young now? Zeke wondered. He wished he could see her. Naomi was probably already on her way to pick her up, and Linda would be dragged away from him again. Naomi had never liked him when they were kids, which Zeke supposed was sort of natural. The Howells didn't exactly boast the most impressive pedigree in Grover's Springs.

And here he was in his dad's old hangout. . . .

His heart filled with dread at the thought of Linda going off with her sister. Maybe Naomi would try to talk her out of whatever attraction she felt for him. He knew she had to feel something. But more than likely, now that Naomi was here, Linda would return to Dallas. Would she want him visiting her there? Would she ever come back here?

Damn, damn, damn! He just didn't want her to leave. Now that they were together, he didn't want to be away from her ever again. Yesterday at his house he'd felt an emotional closeness to her the likes of which he'd never experienced with any woman since Linda. He loved her.

God, yes. Now that the words struck him, he wondered at his thick-headedness in not realizing it before. Why hadn't he let her know that yet? Maybe if he'd been more up-front with his feelings ten years ago, she wouldn't have walked away from him. Instead, they spent too much of their time together clowning around. The word immediately brought to mind the party. Zeke smiled. How could he not love a woman who, when she needed a clown, produced a whole roomful?

Linda sat on the other side of the sheet, still waiting lamely for Zeke to dispute the fact that she wasn't young any longer. Her hopes for such an assurance were plummeting by the second. Okay, so maybe thirty wasn't *young,* but his silence made it sound as if he thought she might as well hang it up.

"Lindy..."

Her head perked up on her shoulders, and she leaned forward. She couldn't tell from Zeke's tone whether what he was going to say was good or bad.

"Have you ever thought..." Zeke swallowed nervously. Then he blurted out, "What if everyone in Grover's Springs had a million dollars except George Warren?"

Linda's heart deflated. She lay back against the bed, which Dwight Doggett had assured her was as clean as the state of Texas would allow. So it was back to the what-if game. She didn't know why she felt so disappointed. "I guess the price of hardware would go up," she answered. Even to her own ears, her words lacked enthusiasm. "What if everyone in town had a million dollars except you, Zeke?"

He laughed. "No biggie. That's how it felt growing up here." They both stared intently at the white sheet for a few moments before he returned, "What if you discovered that Grover's Springs desperately needed a travel agent?"

Linda clucked amusedly. "Fat chance."

Before she could think of a what-if to return to him, Zeke asked quickly, "Linda, I have to know. What if I asked you to marry me?"

"What?" Dwight Doggett cried. He hiked his boots off the desk and brought his leaned-back chair down to the floor with a muffled crash. "Hey, that kind of thing isn't allowed here!"

"Zeke..."

Zeke growled in frustration. He was such a dope, blurting his proposal out like that—as if it were part of their running joke. No wonder Lindy didn't know what to say. After thirteen years he was proposing, and it was through a sheet in a jail.

"Damn!" he cried. Reaching through the bars, he pulled away the stupid sheet so he could see her face.

Linda shot up on her cot and stared at him in shock. "Were you serious?"

"That's what I want to know!" Dwight Doggett cried.

Linda's question pulled the plug on Zeke's welling hopes. Her stone-shocked expression didn't make him feel like celebrating, either. "I meant it," he returned after a moment, drawing back a little, expecting any reaction but a positive one from her now.

"I don't know what to say." Honestly she didn't, except that she was stunned. "Zeke..."

"I know my timing's not so good—"

"Zeke," she interrupted, wishing she could say something to erase the insecurity in his eyes. "I don't know..."

She needed time. Granted, she'd known the man for about fifteen years all told, but everything was happening so fast! One week just wasn't enough to know whether this was it. And she had her work—what would she do about that?

Besides, Zeke hadn't said a word about love, or anything close to it. Maybe coming back to Grover's Springs had simply put him on a nostalgia trip; she would certainly suit nicely as Exhibit *A* on his stroll down memory lane.

In the awkward silence that followed, watching Linda's eyes blinking back a million different desperate reactions to his proposal, Zeke would have given anything to take his words back. He cursed himself for being the worst kind of chump—the sentimental kind. He was even on the verge of telling her he loved her, but what would that do but make her feel even worse?

"Never mind, Lindy." He pulled the sheet back and started pacing in his cell.

The sudden blanket of whiteness in front of her took her breath away.

Never mind? Linda couldn't believe her ears! It was one thing to be ambushed in a jail cell by a sudden proposal. To have it retracted a scant minute later was adding insult to injury.

"Wait just a minute!" In a fury, she stood and reached through the bars, but her shorter arms couldn't reach the sheet. "Officer Doggett, could you give me a hand with this?"

"I don't rightly know if I can," the man said, coming forward with a nervous chuckle. "I ain't never been proposed to."

Linda rolled her eyes in exasperation. "With the sheet," she amended. "Get it out of here."

"I don't approve of this kind of thing going on around here," he said, but when Linda sent a pointed glare his way, the officer did as bidden.

Zeke's stance in front of the bars, arms crossed, staring at her guardedly, exactly mirrored her own. Linda nearly laughed. They certainly didn't look like two people in love.

The sound of a car pulling up outside registered in both their eyes. That amazing rattling could only mean

Naomi's station wagon. Zeke's mouth tightened into a bitter line. "Go home, Lindy."

"What about that proposal, Zeke?" Linda insisted. "Did you mean it?"

His eyes didn't reveal a thing. "What do you think?"

Linda glared at him. "I think you're not being much of a help."

"If you knew how you felt, you wouldn't have any trouble deciding," Zeke bit back.

But he was wrong. It wasn't her feelings she questioned, it was his. Did he love her? Right now he was looking at her as though she were his worst enemy.

Suddenly the door burst open, bringing in a blast of warm summer humid air. Linda shivered, but she wasn't sure whether it had anything to do with the change in temperature. When she looked up, Dwight Doggett was freeing her.

"Your sister's here."

"Linda!" Over Doggett's shoulder, Linda spied Naomi, arms akimbo, looking at her disapprovingly.

"Go on home, Lindy," Zeke repeated.

Those words again...even Zeke's tone reminded her of the one scene of her life that she never wanted to replay. At his petulant pout, Linda realized Zeke should be glad for the iron bars separating them at that instant. If they hadn't been there, she would have throttled him.

"I can't believe this!" Naomi said again, striking just the correct, righteous-big-sister tone.

"Neither can I," Linda mumbled. She spared Zeke only a perfunctory glance as she shuffled toward freedom—freedom she suddenly felt as if she would gladly trade for another ten minutes in jail with Zeke. Unfortunately he looked as miserable and confused as she felt.

"What's happened around here?" Naomi cried, once they were firmly ensconced in the station wagon.

Here it came. Linda burrowed against the passenger-side door and tried to block out the little speech she knew was about to spill from her sister's lips. Despite the hot air blowing on her, she felt clammy and cold and a little bit dizzy.

"First," Naomi began, "I come home to find you in Mrs. Huckabee's tree—"

"That was Zeke," Linda said.

"Zeke Howell!" Her sister slapped her palm against the steering wheel and accidentally tooted the horn. Both of them jumped. "Honestly, Linda, I thought it was safe to leave you alone in the same town with the man for one week. Otherwise I would have warned you to bar the doors or something."

"It *was* safe," Linda countered, pulling the sweater Naomi had brought along more tightly around her. "Nothing happened, Naomi. He was just helping me out with some things." Perhaps it was best not to tell her about the proposal....

"The man whistles and you go running—to jail, in fact. Do not pass Go—"

"I told you," Linda defended wearily, "that was *my* fault."

Naomi ignored her. "Not to mention, the twins are in a state. We finally agreed that they could keep the kittens, but they refused to go to sleep until William told them a story about some warthog. What's that all about?"

Linda smiled woozily, remembering. Had the party been just that afternoon? It seemed like ages ago. Maybe because so much had happened. Her panic after Seth disappeared. Then relief, then shock at seeing Naomi drive up, then abandon. And now this confusion after

Zeke's proposal. It helped to remember him at the party, with the children gathered around him, telling that silly, silly story. Zeke would make a wonderful father.

"Linda?"

Linda snapped to. She hadn't realized that she was so out of it. Really, she felt as if she might faint. Her teeth chattered noisily, and her head felt as though it were filled with thick fluffy cotton balls.

"I don't think you're even listening to me." Naomi clucked her tongue. "What's the matter with you? Are you sick?"

"Sick?" Linda tried but failed to focus in on her sister, who was not even two feet away from her. "Worse than sick," she said, trying to control her slurring words as exhaustion overtook her. "I think I'm in love."

"Oh, my Lord!"

Linda couldn't discern whether Naomi was annoyed by her being in love, or if she'd only just now realized that she was on the verge of blacking out. She would never know. Naomi's startled exclamation was the last thing she heard before she passed out.

Chapter Ten

"Higher on the right."

Zeke let out a sigh of exasperation as he hoisted the sign that said Warren and Howell Hardware a little higher—yet again. Lord, George was fussy!

"I guess that's as good as we're gonna get," George said, squinting up at Zeke standing on a ladder.

Relieved, Zeke pounded in enough nails to hold the sucker for a few millennia. They'd been working at this sign hanging all morning, and he was pooped.

When he stepped back down on solid ground, George jutted out his spidery hand to shake. "Well, partner, how 'bout a drink?"

Without further ado, George shuffled inside, climbed onto his stool, reached under the counter and pulled out an unopened bottle of whiskey and two glasses. "I been waitin' for this day, son. Bought this JD special for the occasion. 'Course, you made me wait longer than I'd planned."

"Go easy on that stuff, George, or you'll be giving away our store before noon."

"Nah," George said dismissively. He poured himself a hearty jiggerful and handed a more modest one to Zeke. "Here's to partnership."

Zeke lifted his glass and thought gloomily about Linda. Partnership. They would have made great life partners, but apparently she still didn't see it that way. Not that he'd heard from her—every time he went by to see her, Naomi fended him off with the excuse that Linda was sick. He'd sent flowers, but had still received no word. Maybe she was just sick of *him*.

"Are you still moping about that woman?" George asked wearily.

"I'm sorry, George," Zeke replied, putting down his untouched glass.

"That woman has never been anything but trouble!" George exclaimed. Then he added, "I think you ought to marry her."

Zeke's eyes widened with surprise. "You what?"

"Sure! Nothing wrong with a little trouble every once in a while. Look at Vera."

"Vera Huckabee? George, you two aren't—"

"And what's the matter with that?" George cut him off with his most ornery tone. "Me and Vera go way back. Further than you and that Potter woman. And if she plays her cards right, Vera Huckabee might maneuver this confirmed old bachelor to the altar in time for a June wedding."

Zeke shook his head slowly in disbelief. "I never knew."

"Humph." George got out his pipe and lit it. "A retired man can't spend every day fishing, you know. He needs somebody to talk to—and so do you!"

"I've talked with Linda," Zeke said. "We've talked and talked—we're perfect for each other. Only trouble is, when I asked her to marry me, she looked at me like I'd sprouted two heads."

"You must not have done it right," George said. Apparently, now that he'd revealed his liaison with Vera Huckabee, the old man was comfortable in his role of love expert. "When did you pop the question?"

"The other night," Zeke answered vaguely.

"Which night?"

"You know, before you came to get me."

"In the jail? You asked a woman to marry you in the jail?" George let out a snorting cackle. "I thought Dwight was pulling my leg about that."

"He told you?" Zeke shifted uncomfortably.

"What do you expect? The man's lonelier than the Maytag repairman watching over that empty slammer. Your visit there was big news."

"Well, it doesn't matter," Zeke said despondently. "She said no."

"Flat-out, dead-certain no?" George's eyebrows shot up speculatively.

Zeke thought for a moment. "It was more of an implied, too-shocked-to-answer no."

"Doesn't count!"

"Maybe not to you, old man," Zeke bit out. "But you're not the one who stuck his neck out."

"Is that all you're worried about—your neck?" George laughed. "Maybe you should try putting some heart into it."

Zeke let out a short laugh. "That's good, coming from you."

"Maybe it's true I haven't led the most lovey-dovey kind of life. But I've got a woman to talk to." He winked slyly. "One with a good view of the Grover's Springs municipal park. Especially that fountain."

Zeke's head, which had been hanging despondently, snapped up. "Did you call the police?"

"Which time?"

Zeke folded his arms across his chest. "You old cuss."

George cackled. "The point is, you gotta follow your heart sometime, Zeke. Take it from me, it's a lot less lonely if you start young."

"I did. When I was in high school." He'd loved Linda since then, he knew that for certain. But ever since he'd met her, he'd felt as if he was chasing something he couldn't have.

"It's one thing for you to say I should follow my heart, George," Zeke said regretfully. "Given my history with Linda, I'd be a masochist to follow your little gem of wisdom."

George shrugged. "Just wanted to help."

"Thanks." Thinking better of it, Zeke slugged down the little glass of whiskey on the counter. "Here's to you, partner."

With or without Linda, he had roots now. A house and a store with his name hanging over the sidewalk in big letters—citizens didn't get any more fine and upstanding than that. This was where he belonged now. If Linda changed her mind about his proposal, Zeke thought stubbornly, she would know where to find him.

Now all he could do was pray she changed her mind....

By Thursday Linda felt well enough to take the twins to the vet with Hippo and the new kitten, Blotch, for his shots. If she was honest with herself, she would have to say that she was also well enough to drive back to Dallas. But for some reason she just hadn't mustered the get-up-and-go to do it. Leaving, actually packing her bags and driving back to Dallas, seemed so final. She wanted to put it off for as long as possible.

To get to the vet's, Linda had to drive the car through downtown Grover's Springs, which consisted of about four blocks of old store buildings, a few empty; although some of the businesses housed there were still managing to hang on. But the area was a boon for the twins, whose favorite car game at the moment was What-does-that-sign-say?

"That says it's a fabric store," Linda said in answer to their question.

"Mommy goes there," Seth said smartly. "Saul got in trouble for hiding in the cloth last time."

In the rearview mirror, Linda saw Saul's face turn a pinkish hue. "Not very bad trouble," he said in his own defense.

But Seth was already bored with the fabric store. "What does that sign say, Aunt Lindy?"

"Pharmacy," Linda answered.

"What's that?" the twins asked in unison.

As she pulled up to one of the town's five stoplights, Linda said, "That's where they sell drugs."

"That's a bad place," Seth whispered to Saul.

Linda was trying to think of a good way to explain the difference between medicinal drugs and narcotics to five-year-olds when Seth pointed again.

"What's that sign say?"

She looked over and was about to reply that it was the hardware store, but her gaze became glued to the sign itself. Warren and Howell Hardware, the hand-painted placard read. Howell? Since when had Zeke become a shopkeeper?

"What's it say?" Seth demanded again.

"Green light!" Saul shouted from the back seat as a car horn honked impatiently behind them.

"Green means go," Seth put in for Linda's benefit.

Linda shook her head and her car lurched forward. As they passed the hardware store, she glanced again at the sign, wondering for a second if she had perhaps just seen a mirage. But she hadn't.

"She never did say what that one was," Seth observed.

"That must be a really bad place," his brother whispered back.

"That's the hardware store," Linda supplied, brought temporarily out of her brooding. "Remember? We were there just last week." She marveled at her own words. Just last week? It seemed ages ago now.

"Oh, yeah," Seth said. Linda could tell he was already looking around for another sign to question her about.

Luckily, they were almost at the vet's. Linda was glad for the diversion. For the next half hour, she ostensibly concentrated on making the twins keep Hippo and Blotch inside their box and explaining the necessity of having a strange man poke their kittens with a large needle.

But all she could really think about was that sign. Finally, Zeke had taken George up on his offer. But why now? she wondered suspiciously. If he'd intended to send her a message, it was coming through loud and clear. Zeke Howell had settled in Grover's Springs, and apparently planned to stay with or without her.

Now the question was, what were *her* plans?

"Linda, I've got the greatest news."

Linda flopped down onto the couch with Naomi's old

clunky phone and, since her sister was nowhere in sight, propped her feet on the coffee table. "Okay, shoot," she told Jane.

"The properties manager of the location you wanted in Houston just called with an offer. It's half what they were offering before."

In contrast to Jane's voice, which was brimming over with enthusiasm, Linda felt her body sag into Naomi's cushions. "That's great," she murmured.

"*Great?*" Jane the go-getter seemed a little frustrated by her boss's lack of response. "It's terrific! This is the opportunity you've been waiting for!"

Was it really? Linda thought with wonder. Had she truly been working and striving for ten years for the moment when she could buy a lot in a shopping center in Houston? It sounded anticlimactic to her now, to say the least.

"I'll have to think about it," she answered listlessly.

"*Think about it?* Linda, have you gone insane?" Jane let out a sigh of frustration. "This is about the hunk, isn't it?"

"No, it's not," Linda replied quickly. Who was she trying to kid? With a sigh, she said, "Yes, it is."

"Trust me, those old flame things never work out. My sister Leslie fell in love all over again with her high school sweetheart, only to find out that he'd just been released from San Quentin."

Linda laughed. "The only time Zeke was in jail, I was with him."

"You, in jail? When was that?"

"Saturday."

Silence followed that admission. Finally Jane cleared her throat. "Listen, why don't I call you back later, after you've had time to think about this. You can't stay away from your business forever, you know—I'm surprised you made it this long. You need us like we need you."

After hanging up, Linda thought about Jane's last words for a long time. If she'd learned anything in the past week, it was that On the Wing didn't really need her. Was the reverse also true?

Her head felt muddled and woozy. Maybe she was still sicker than she knew. Or maybe she was merely depressed because she knew now that neither her business nor Zeke needed her.... Of course, there was at least cold comfort in the fact that she'd never actually fallen in love with her travel agency, or worse, expected it to love her back. Zeke, however, was another matter entirely.

Linda stumbled through the kitchen. At the table, Saul and Seth were having an afternoon snack of milk and cupcakes. They regarded her with large worried eyes.

"Are you sad, Aunt Lindy?" Seth asked.

"No," Linda lied. "I'm just going out onto the porch for some fresh air.

She pushed through the screen door and sat herself on a step. Roses and other flowers filled her gaze with their jaunty blooms, but the sight did little to lift her spirits. They only reminded her of Zeke's spectacular backyard, and the time they'd shared there. Linda buried her face in her hands and tried to bite back tears. She was behaving like a child again, which was foolish.

He didn't love her. He'd watched her walk away twice. A word would have stopped her, but he didn't have the desire to stop her. He'd never really given her a sign that he loved her. Not all those years ago, and certainly not now. All he'd done was propose to her—in a cold jail cell. Probably, as she'd suspected at the time, on a whim.

If only she'd reciprocated on a whim! she thought now. So maybe it would have been a mistake—at least she would have had the chance to find out. She was beginning to think the rash, wild side of her that she had left in Grover's Springs hadn't been so harmful after all. Now, without it, all she had to look forward to was thirty-five years of scheduling other people's vacations.

Behind her, the screen door opened and closed, and the sound of two pairs of little sneaker-encased feet coming toward her followed. Moments after their shuffling stopped near her, Linda felt a tiny finger tap on her shoulder.

She looked up to see the concerned faces of Seth and Saul looming close. From behind his back, Saul produced a chocolate cupcake.

"It's happy food," Seth explained.

Although she could have cried like a baby at the boys' gesture, Linda instead took the sticky cupcake from Seth's small hands. "Thanks," she said as the two settled themselves down on either side of her. Somehow, the trusting warmth of their presence lifted her spirits where those flowers had failed. Or maybe they were right about that cupcake being happy food. Either way, she felt her dark mood lifting.

"We had the best birthday ever, Aunt Lindy."

Linda looked skeptically at Seth. "You did?"

"I want a party again next year," Saul said. "Will you dress up as a clown again?"

She turned to her other nephew in disbelief. He'd had a miserable time at the party!

"Will Zeke come as a clown next year, too?" Seth asked.

"I miss Zeke," his brother added sadly.

Linda ruffled Saul's head just the way Zeke so often had. "Me, too."

"Why doesn't he come inside anymore?"

Linda blinked. "Inside?"

"He used to talk to Mommy about you, but now he just sits in his truck most of the time."

"Doesn't he like us anymore?"

"He hasn't come inside since he brought the flowers. And those were only for you," Seth added scornfully.

Linda couldn't believe her ears. She'd been watching those flowers wilt all week, but had never thought to ask Naomi who they'd come from. Maybe Naomi had told her they were from Zeke while she was sick and she just didn't remember.

Her heartbeat started picking up. And he'd been coming by! Asking about her!

"Are you glad Zeke's gone, Aunt Lindy?" Saul asked.

Through a blur, Linda focused in on her nephews' dear faces. Suddenly everything seemed more dear to her—more dear and more fantastically wonderful. Zeke cared, he had to. The stubborn man was just too proud to say so!

"Of course not," she answered. "Why would you think that I'd be glad he's gone?"

"Because you're smiling!"

Linda laughed out loud. Smiling? She felt as if her whole body were smiling. Impulsively she gathered up her two nephews, one on each side, and gave them the hug of a lifetime. "You two are the greatest kids in the whole wide world, you know that?"

Seth beamed up at her. "Yeah, we know."

Her car must have steered itself toward the hardware store, because Linda found herself there without even remembering putting the key in the ignition.

She got out and approached the store cautiously. Now that the moment of reckoning had come, she was a little more wary. Looking again at the sign boasting Zeke's name in waterproof, permanent letters, she took a deep breath and pressed on through the door. Linda was disappointed to see Zeke nowhere in evidence. Somehow, the possibility of his not being there had never occurred to her.

At the jangling of the doorbell, however, George Warren looked over at her from his usual perch and smiled. "Thought I'd see you around here sooner or later. Sooner, more than likely." He chuckled, then frowned and waved at her with his pipe. "Zeke's not here."

Linda's shoulders sagged. "Do you know where he is?" She was already turning for the door.

"You just wait a cotton-pickin' minute, missy. I've got a bone to pick with you," George said. "You've got my boy so tangled up in knots that he's taken two weeks to work on a simple roof-repair job."

Her head snapped up. "He's at the Bledsoes'?" Quickly she registered something else the man had said. "Tied in knots, did you say?"

"Thought that might get your attention. Old Zeke seems to think he's stuck his neck out far enough where you're concerned."

"His neck?" Linda huffed indignantly. "Why isn't he more concerned with his heart?"

"That's what I said!"

Linda stared at George in slack-jawed surprise. "You did?"

"Yup. Then he said you'd already stomped all over his poor little heart, or some such nonsense."

"I never did!" Linda exclaimed.

George shook his head dismissively. "The boy's not thinking clearly. Love bug's bitten him harder this time than it did after you two fools ran off to Mexico. Or Waco."

"Love?" Linda's fists dug into her hips in scolding imitation of the stance she'd seen Naomi take so many times. "Thirteen years ago? Are you sure?"

As the old man took a fortifying suck on his pipe, Linda could see the honesty in his eyes. George wasn't just concerned about finding a partner to go fishing; he loved Zeke as much as she did. Nearly. She had a hard time believing anyone could manage to love Zeke more than she did.

"I'm two hundred percent positive," George said. "And I'm almost as positive that Zeke realizes he's made a mistake in not saying so."

Linda smiled at the man for what had to be the first time in her life. Maybe she was in love with the whole wide world today. "George, you've got to be the pokiest matchmaker on this planet!"

Seconds later she was back in her car, speeding toward Mulberry Street, where the Bledsoes lived. But as fast as she was driving, her thoughts were racing even faster. George said Zeke loved her! It echoed through her mind again and again.

Just as she turned the corner onto Mulberry, a glance in her rearview mirror made her rethink being in love with the *entire* world. Dwight Doggett's patrol car was bearing down on her, his lights flashing. Of all the luck!

She slammed on her brakes and jumped out of her car.

"Where you going in such a hurry?" Doggett drawled as he ambled forward. "I been chasing you for fifteen blocks!"

"You have?" Good grief—she'd been so intent on getting to Zeke she hadn't even noticed a policeman on her tail!

"Closest thing to a high-speed chase this town's ever seen," Doggett said enthusiastically. "I'm afraid I'll have to take you in, Lindy. You sure have livened up the old Springs, though."

Anxiously Linda scanned up and down the street. This *was* the right street, wasn't it? "Officer," she pleaded, "I really don't have time for this."

Dwight Doggett's eyes widened with unmitigated joy. "Are you resisting arrest? Are you really?" The eager cop was already reaching for his shiny, unused cuffs.

"No!" Linda cried. "I swear, I'm a law-abiding citizen!" Just then she spotted Zeke's truck parked in a driveway two houses down. Suddenly a loud piercing whistle echoed down the street and both Linda and Doggett looked heavenward.

"Zeke!" Linda cried. In a split second, she was dashing toward the Bledsoes' house.

"Hey, wait a minute!" Officer Doggett took off after her.

Linda streaked across two lawns and, before she could think better of it, dashed up a ladder to the rooftop Zeke was standing on. Dumbfounded, Zeke gave her a hand up and stared at her for a moment before breaking into a wide sexy grin. "Glad you dropped up."

Linda's sandaled feet struggled for purchase on the slanted rooftop. "Oh, my Lord!" she cried, looking down for the first time. She repeated the exclamation when she saw Doggett staring up at her.

"You'd better get back down here!" the officer bellowed happily.

Looking back at Zeke and gathering her wits, Linda remembered what she was doing on the roof in the first place. "Keep your shirt on, Doggett," she called back down, keeping her eyes on Zeke. "I've got a few words to say to this man."

"Me?" Zeke's smile had faded, but he appeared unfazed by the whole situation. "What could you say to me now that you couldn't have last week?"

"Just this. You love me," Linda announced flatly. "You loved me way back when, too, but you were too stupid and proud to say so." Rewarded with Zeke's stunned expression, she moved forward and added, "And don't try to deny it, either, because I have a witness."

"Who?" Zeke asked, reaching forward to steady her in her mincing progress across the tiles.

"George Warren."

"George is a liar. Always has been." His eyes glinted with challenge, and a little electric thrill zipped through her as he held her firmly in front of him.

"The twins said you've been coming by the house."

"To check on you."

"Because you love me," she countered. "And you know I love you."

At her words, his grip on her arms tightened possessively. "No, I didn't know that."

"Well, now you do. I love you, Zeke." She looked up at him through moist eyes. "So what are you going to do about it?"

"Just this." His mouth descended on hers and his arms wrapped tightly about her. For a few blissful moments, Linda felt as if she were literally in the clouds.

Finally having what she'd wanted for so agonizingly long made her dizzy with happiness.

A little buzz rang through the air.

"What's that?" Zeke asked, pulling back.

"My beeper again," Linda said, taking the little plastic device from her belt. "Jane wanted to talk to me more about opening an office in Houston."

For a second, Zeke looked honestly stricken. "Are you going to do that?"

"No," Linda answered right away. "I might be able to launch a satellite office in Tyler, though...."

"Then I guess we can launch this," Zeke said, laughing as he took her beeper and tossed it off the roof.

Startled, Linda followed her beeper's arc through the sky with her arm, throwing her balance off. She weaved and swayed before Zeke caught her.

"Ouch! Hey, what is this?" Officer Doggett held up the beeper, which had nicked him on the shoulder.

"It's my lifeline!" Linda cried helplessly.

"Let me be your lifeline, sweetheart," Zeke said. "I'll smother you in beepers."

"That kind of talk could turn a girl's head," Linda threw back at him saucily.

He bent down to kiss her again, but stopped his lips centimeters from hers. "Marry me, Lindy," he urged in a husky whisper. "We'll drive to Louisiana—"

"We've wasted too much time already—"

"Today," Zeke agreed, then sealed his intention with a kiss.

They held each other for several long moments, savoring the prospect of a lifetime of shared happiness. Until Linda suddenly remembered a hitch in the proceedings....

She glanced down at Officer Doggett, who was twirling his pair of handcuffs on one hand. A small but intently curious crowd had gathered around the Bledsoes' house to watch the show being played out on the roof. Linda moaned in dismay.

"I'm afraid the nuptials will have to wait," she whispered to Zeke.

"Do you have any better ideas for how to spend a sultry summer afternoon?" he said as he nuzzled her neck playfully, oblivious to their audience.

"How about posting bail?"

Suddenly Zeke's lips cut off their journey to her collarbone. He straightened with a sigh and gave the crowd below them a little salute. "We're getting married!" he cried down to them, and he hugged Linda's waist affectionately.

"It's about time!" Vera Huckabee cried back from below. She sent both of them a sly wink.

"And I guess it's about time for me to be hauled off to jail," Linda said, shaking her head in disbelief. Zeke gave her a hand as she began to descend the ladder. "You will bail me out, won't you?"

Zeke kneeled down on the edge of the roof so that they were staring at each other face-to-face. "Always. Till death do us part."

And to prove his sincerity—or maybe because he just couldn't get enough of her—he sealed the bargain with a long, loving kiss.

*   *   *   *   *

Get Ready to be Swept Away by
Silhouette's Spring Collection

Abduction
& Seduction

These passion-filled stories explore both the dangerous
desires of men and the seductive powers of women.
Written by three of our most celebrated authors, they are
sure to capture your hearts.

Diana Palmer
Brings us a spin-off of her Long, Tall Texans series

Joan Johnston
Crafts a beguiling Western romance

Rebecca Brandewyne
New York Times bestselling author
makes a smashing contemporary debut

Available in March at your favorite retail outlet.

ABSED

Take 4 bestselling love stories FREE

Plus get a FREE surprise gift!

Special Limited-time Offer

Mail to Silhouette Reader Service™

> 3010 Walden Avenue
> P.O. Box 1867
> Buffalo, N.Y. 14269-1867

YES! Please send me 4 free Silhouette Romance™ novels and my free surprise gift. Then send me 6 brand-new novels every month, which I will receive months before they appear in bookstores. Bill me at the low price of $2.19 each plus 25¢ delivery and applicable sales tax, if any.* That's the complete price and—compared to the cover prices of $2.75 each—quite a bargain! I understand that accepting the books and gift places me under no obligation ever to buy any books. I can always return a shipment and cancel at any time. Even if I never buy another book from Silhouette, the 4 free books and the surprise gift are mine to keep forever.

215 BPA ANRP

Name	(PLEASE PRINT)	
Address	Apt. No.	
City	State	Zip

This offer is limited to one order per household and not valid to present Silhouette Romance™ subscribers. *Terms and prices are subject to change without notice. Sales tax applicable in N.Y.

USROM-94R   ©1990 Harlequin Enterprises Limited

HE'S MORE THAN A MAN,
HE'S ONE OF OUR

FATHER IN THE MIDDLE
Phyllis Halldorson

Clay Rutledge needed a new nanny and like a miracle,
Tamara Houston was there. But little did Clay know that
beautiful Tamara was a mother on a mission—and that his
adopted daughter was the child she'd once given up....

Look for *Father in the Middle* by Phyllis Halldorson—available
in February from Silhouette Romance.

Fall in love with our Fabulous Fathers!

Silhouette
R O M A N C E™

FF295

Coming in February from

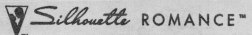

✦ _Silhouette_ ROMANCE™

Sister Switch

by
Carolyn Zane

When twin sisters switch identities, mischief, mayhem—and romance—are sure to follow!

UNWILLING WIFE
(FEB. '95 #1063)

Erica Brant agreed to take her sister's place as nanny for two rambunctious children. But she never considered that their handsome single father would want to make *her* his new bride!

WEEKEND WIFE
(MAY '95 #1082)

When a sexy stranger begged Emily Brant to pose as his wife for the weekend, it was an offer she couldn't resist. But what happens when she discovers he wants more than just a pretend marriage?

Don't miss the fun as the Brant sisters discover that trading places can lead to more than they'd ever imagined. SISTER SWITCH—only from Silhouette Romance!

SSD

Those Harris boys are back in book three of...

WEDDING WAGER

by Sandra Steffen

Three sexy, single brothers bet they'll never say "I do."
But the Harris boys are about to discover their vows of bachelor-
hood don't stand a chance against the forces of love!

You met Mitch in BACHELOR DADDY #1028 (8/94) and Kyle in
BACHELOR AT THE WEDDING #1045 (11/94). Now it's time for
brother Taylor to take the marriage plunge in—

EXPECTANT BACHELOR #1056 (1/95): When Gina Jenson sets
out to seduce the handsome Taylor, he's in for the surprise of his
life. Because Gina wants him to father her child!

If you missed the first books in Sandra Steffen's WEDDING WAGER series, *Bachelor Daddy* (Silhouette Romance #1028), or *Bachelor at the Wedding* (Silhouette Romance #1045), order your copy now by sending your name, address, zip or postal code, along with a check or money order (please do not send cash) for $2.75 ($3.25 in Canada), plus 75¢ postage and handling ($1.00 in Canada), payable to Silhouette Books, to:

In the U.S.	In Canada
Silhouette Books	Silhouette Books
3010 Walden Ave.	P.O. Box 636
P.O. Box 9077	Fort Erie, Ontario
Buffalo, NY 14269-9077	L2A 5X3

*Please specify book title(s) with your order.
 Canadian residents add applicable federal and provincial taxes.

SRSS3

The miracle of love is waiting to be discovered in Duncan, Oklahoma! Arlene James takes you there in her miniseries, THIS SIDE OF HEAVEN. Look for book four in February:

THE ROGUE WHO CAME TO STAY

Rodeo champ Griff Shaw had come home to Duncan to heal when he found pretty single mom Joan Burton and her adorable daughter living in his house! Griff wasn't about to turn Joan and her little girl out, but did Joan dare share a roof with this rugged rogue?

Available in February, from

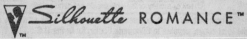

SOH

SILHOUETTE... Where Passion Lives

Don't miss these Silhouette favorites by some of our most
distinguished authors! And now you can receive a discount by
ordering two or more titles!

SD#05786	QUICKSAND by Jennifer Greene	$2.89	☐
SD#05795	DEREK by Leslie Guccione	$2.99	☐
SD#05818	NOT JUST ANOTHER PERFECT WIFE by Robin Elliott	$2.99	☐
IM#07505	HELL ON WHEELS by Naomi Horton	$3.50	☐
IM#07514	FIRE ON THE MOUNTAIN by Marion Smith Collins	$3.50	☐
IM#07559	KEEPER by Patricia Gardner Evans	$3.50	☐
SSE#09879	LOVING AND GIVING by Gina Ferris	$3.50	☐
SSE#09892	BABY IN THE MIDDLE by Marie Ferrarella	$3.50 u.s. $3.99 can.	☐
SSE#09902	SEDUCED BY INNOCENCE by Lucy Gordon	$3.50 u.s. $3.99 can.	☐
SR#08952	INSTANT FATHER by Lucy Gordon	$2.75	☐
SR#08984	AUNT CONNIE'S WEDDING by Marie Ferrarella	$2.75	☐
SR#08990	JILTED by Joleen Daniels	$2.75	☐

(limited quantities available on certain titles)

AMOUNT	$_____
DEDUCT: 10% DISCOUNT FOR 2+ BOOKS	$_____
POSTAGE & HANDLING	$_____
($1.00 for one book, 50¢ for each additional)	
APPLICABLE TAXES*	$_____
TOTAL PAYABLE	$_____
(check or money order—please do not send cash)	

To order, complete this form and send it, along with a check or money order
for the total above, payable to Silhouette Books, to: **In the U.S.:** 3010 Walden
Avenue, P.O. Box 9077, Buffalo, NY 14269-9077; **In Canada:** P.O. Box 636,
Fort Erie, Ontario, L2A 5X3.

Name:_____

Address:_____ City:_____

State/Prov.:_____ Zip/Postal Code:_____

*New York residents remit applicable sales taxes.
Canadian residents remit applicable GST and provincial taxes.   SBACK-DF

Silhouette®